Invaders the Invasion Has Begun

Francisco Angulo de Lafuente

Published by Francisco Angulo de Lafuente, 2023.

INVADERS THE INVASION HAS BEGUN

First edition. August 20, 2023.

ISBN: 979-8223917441

Written by Francisco Angulo de Lafuente.

Table of Contents

INVADERS

The invasion has begun
Jellyfish Invasion
INVADERS The invasion has begun
For years we have feared an alien invasion.
But what if they were already here?

WARNING

IF YOU ARE ONE OF THOSE people who reads a book once a year hoping it will change your life: Don't read this book, that's what the Bible, the Quran or Buddhist Mantras are for.

If your neighbor has already been abducted by aliens and you are looking for a practical guide to fight them: Stop watching Ancient Aliens.

If you think Belén Esteban is the leader of an alien race planning to take over the earth: You are right! For years she has used television to lobotomize viewers, cancelling their will...

If your psychiatrist gives you endless pills and authorizes you to use marijuana to treat depression: That's not your psychiatrist, it's your neighborhood drug dealer!

This novel is not based on real events.

Do not believe a word you read below.

Prologue

They came without warning - strange jellyfish-like creatures that flooded our oceans and beaches by the millions. At first they seemed a mere curiosity, these alien visitors glowing faintly purple as they pulsed through the waves. Tourists gathered to marvel at their graceful forms, children delighted in their squishy texture. We should have been warier from the start.

The first victim was a scuba diver, stung by the tentacles of an unknown species. Within hours a raging fever set in, soon followed by violent delirium. He became the index case of the epidemic as the mysterious neurotoxin spread rapidly from human to human.

Chaos erupted within days as the infected hordes - crazed and cannibalistic - overwhelmed authorities. Cities descended into anarchy, society teetered on the brink of collapse. Our leaders responded with lethal force and martial law, to little avail. For the jellyfish were only the heralds of a full-scale invasion from below, one that threatened to wipe humanity from the face of the Earth.

With INVADERS, Francisco Angulo has crafted a genuinely frightening and all-too-plausible doomsday scenario, underpinned by rapid-fire action and tantalizing scientific speculation. Part Michael Crichton and part Stephen King, Angulo's vision of an alien-engineered apocalypse will have you watching the waters with wary eyes long after you've turned the final page.

I wanted to write a novel in the style of those fantastic stories that appeared in those old American magazines for geeks: Amazing Stories, Science Fiction, Infinity, etc... A novel without pretense, with the sole purpose of entertaining and of course with the idea of having fun during the creative process. With everything going on and all the media talking to us about the crisis, I thought we'd have to have some fun with something, at least for now reading and writing is free...

INVADERS
The invasion has begun
Jellyfish Invasion

It all started when after another day of diving testing one of my Nautilus Diver Kit prototypes, when I got home I started feeling sick. I took my temperature and was able to confirm what I suspected, I had quite a fever. I felt very dizzy and was starting to get nauseous. My back was burning, I felt an itching sensation going up to my neck. Looking in the mirror I was frightened to see the strong skin reaction, I had lots of very fine red streaks all over my back, a very intense bright red, like glowing hot metal. I remembered that during the dive I saw a school of small jellyfish, but I didn't give it much thought. It was late, so I applied body oil all over my back as best I could despite the difficulty. Then I drank a glass of milk and got into bed. I spent the worst night of my life, shivering from fever, cold sweats and a series of terrifying nightmares. When I got up to go pee, I could barely stand, I got to the bathroom holding onto the walls so as not to lose my balance. I don't like taking medications, but this time I looked in my wallet where I always keep some Aspirin, they say it's an obsolete drug and Nolotil, Acetaminophen or Dipyrone are better, personally I prefer traditional remedies, products that have been tested for decades. The acetylsalicylic acid contained in willow leaves has been used by humanity for over 2,000 years. I struggled for twenty minutes not to throw up. I called the clinic and went there first thing in the morning. My doctor wasn't there, a lady doctor was replacing him, truthfully I didn't care, since I only go to the doctor's office once every two or three years, I barely know him. The doctor had a lifeless gaze, black eyes without light, her voice was similar to an automated reader, sharp words one after the other, as if they were following a script. If she hadn't been standing in front of me, I would have said I was talking to Siri. At that moment I was feeling so bad that I didn't think about it, she prescribed me an ointment with corticosteroid hormones. When I got up to leave, I caught a brief glimpse of some reddish marks on her uncovered neck, similar to those on my back. As if wanting to hide something, she immediately pulled up the white collar of her lab coat. I got home staggering, my forehead burning, I quickly applied the cream and got back into bed. The nightmares returned shaking me violently, I was delirious, unable to differentiate dreams from reality, everything intertwined. I somehow got the three or four Aspirin I had left into my mouth and finally lost consciousness. I woke up three days later, alarms sounding in the streets and grunts and screams everywhere. That's when I began to suspect something was not right, something was happening. I was very weak and my tongue felt stiff, I needed to drink and eat to recover. I looked out the window and saw people running back and forth in terror. There was a car crashed into a storefront, a van overturned in the middle of the street. Sirens and alarms sounded, from businesses, vehicles and also firefighters, police and ambulances.

Before putting myself in danger by going down to the street to find out what was happening, I thought it would be safest to turn on the news, but the TV wasn't working, I couldn't tune into any channels. "NO SIGNAL". That innocuous message in the middle of a black screen terrified me. The second thing I did was look for my cell phone, I had left it disconnected and it was off without a battery charge. I plugged it into the charger and nervously waited for it to restart. I had no coverage, I held it up high and spun it around in circles, but it was all in vain. On the desk in my room was my small laptop, through which I got some information. Although the online news sites did not work, nor email. I could only access some old pages saved in the cache of pirate servers. I found a lot of information talking about the mysterious plague of jellyfish. The news referred to the mission of the Hespérides vessel.

HIGHLIGHTED NEWS August 12th
New jellyfish plague invades our coasts

Several bathers have been hospitalized after jellyfish stings. These previously unknown episodes are becoming habitual every year around this time, while the jellyfish plague is starting to become something we are getting used to, it is also true that this year's outbreak has broken all records. In the past they were small specimens, annoying but not very harmful, but now there are various species, some very large, like the recently discovered one named Giganteacolosalis by scientists, a gigantic size species as its name indicates. This jellyfish specimen does not seem to have any venom, although its enormous size makes it very dangerous for humans, especially for those who practice water sports, since its gelatinous and sticky body the size of a medium boat, can easily trap a person preventing them from swimming or getting out of the water, as if they were caught in a spider web. But beware, because among our new visitors are two certainly dangerous species, one the size of a thumb, contains a neurotoxic venom a thousand times more lethal than that of the king cobra.

Authorities have declared a red alert on all our beaches and bathing and water activities are prohibited until further notice.

INVADERS
The invasion has begun
Jellyfish Invasion
Day 1

The ship departed from the port of Santander and many family members and curious onlookers came out to bid farewell to the ship, something that is traditional for these types of long voyages, even more so for a navy vessel. The crew in command was military and the civilians were researchers, doctors and teachers. Dr. Garcia did not come out on deck, she stayed unpacking in her cabin. Maria Garcia was a redhead with a lot of freckles, her coppery orange hair combed with a center part and pulled up in a bun. Her eyes were an indeterminate light color, a mix of green and amber tones. Despite her leadership skills and the utmost importance of her research, she was a cheerful woman, always wore a pretty smile. A decent sized room, with a bed, built-in closet, desk and private bathroom with shower, something that is not usually available in the rest of the crew quarters, of course she was the one leading the mission this time, left behind were many other trips on shabby boats that didn't even have running water. She still remembered some of those expeditions, one of them sailing down the Amazon River, where the entire crew contracted acute gastroenteritis. Maria was very restless, she sensed this was not going to be an easy mission, and it wasn't just about the responsibility of the position she held, the latest biopsies done in the lab on new specimens, unknown to science, had left her full of doubts and fears. Far from finding answers, the investigation led to more questions, there were hundreds of issues to resolve. She didn't know why but something told her not to go north, not to follow the jellyfish to their spawning ground.

HIGHLIGHTED NEWS August 30th
The Hespérides goes jellyfish hunting

The oceanographic vessel Hespérides sets sail with Dr. Maria Garcia on board, our most renowned biologist is in charge of leading the Cnidarian mission. The ship heads towards the Arctic Ocean, believed to be where the jellyfish come from. In the crystal clear waters of the North Pole is where the eggs of these creatures germinate releasing pelagic larvae, planulae that attach to the ocean floor when they find a suitable substrate. They then move towards warmer areas, where they grow and proliferate, but their life cycle is completely unknown, it is still unclear how, when and where they reproduce. The Hespérides will provide answers to these and many other questions.

INVADERS
The invasion has begun
Jellyfish Invasion
Day 2

A dense fog covered the ship early in the morning, it was thin and gray, similar to the smoke from a forest fire, but as the day progressed it turned white and dense, it seemed they were in the middle of a snowstorm, the air was so dense and cold it was hard to breathe. There were few people walking on deck, only some military crew members, who had the mission to go out every so often to check that everything was in order.

That same morning a meeting had been called in which Maria gave instructions to the different research teams, assigning them a task, work schedules, meals and rest times. A few hours later they were already working in the lab. They had not yet collected water or specimen samples, but they brought with them those found on the coast. It was a good time to study them in depth. At least that's what the doctor thought, she spent the whole day scalpel in hand, sectioning thin sheets of each specimen to examine them closely under the microscope.

"Look Tim! It's amazing the strange appendages this specimen has. Can you take a look and tell me what you think?" She called without taking her eyes off the microscope.

"I'll give you my opinion on one condition: Tonight we're setting up a poker game and we don't want the captain to find out... You know, the soldiers are prohibited from gambling while on duty."

Timothy Hannan, was an Englishman, from London. At 32, he was somewhat overweight, after his recent divorce, he had spent the last month eating spicy chicken wings with french fries. He was also freckled, but unlike Maria, his skin was very white and red in the face, his hair was straw yellow. He spoke Spanish with a terrible accent, almost no one understood what he said, so with Dr. Garcia he usually spoke English.

"What time are you planning to start?"

"We'll meet at nine right after dinner in the conference room."

"On one condition: I want to participate too."

"I hope you don't pluck us all like last time..."

Dr. Maria Garcia's name sounded over the PA system, she was being summoned to the bridge, the captain needed to consult with her about some things. Tim stayed behind studying the unusual specimen. As soon as he looked at it under the microscope, he frowned in surprise at what he was seeing.

"Damn it, fuck!"

He quickly disinfected his hands with alcohol and, armed with a scalpel, speared the jellyfish as if it were a kebab, while it writhed in spasms.

Commander Bruce's Flight Logs

The Model

Spring coming to an end and the fields still green with growing cereal, showed tall ears of grain swayed by the gentle breeze. The warm air almost like summer but denser and more humid. The cereal fields stretched as far as I could see. I stood in the middle of a dirt road from which I would launch it. I started the electric motor of the model I had so lovingly built. A white balsa wood sailboat motorized with a Kyosho and nickel-cadmium batteries. I released the beautiful motor sailer that seemed impatient to get out of my hands and take flight. The plane took off without difficulty, soon reaching a good cruising speed. I was twelve years old and inexperienced at flying scale model airplanes.

I left the transmitter on the ground while launching it. A big mistake, because the slightest imbalance in the small plane could destabilize it and make it crash. Luckily when I picked up the transmitter from the ground and looked ahead, the graceful model maintained a low flight about fifty centimeters over the wheat spikes. The white airplane with a wingspan of one meter eighty flew over the field of green spikes as if guided by rails, in perfect balance. Seeing it glide on the wind hypnotized me. Before I knew it, it was very far away, almost beyond my sight and very likely beyond the range of my two-channel Futaba transmitter. So without thinking twice I pulled the controls towards me and the plane went up vertically like a rocket. After the climb it began to lose speed until it almost stopped in the air. I then had to operate the controls again to get the nose to drop before it stalled. It was at that moment that I remembered the hobby store seller's offer to teach me how to fly it. I lived that experience as if I had been inside the cockpit, piloting the airplane myself.

Old models are nothing like current ones, made in one piece. It used to take weeks or months to build them, in balsa wood parts, following the original aircraft plans. Despite what it may seem, even today airplanes are still manufactured in wood, although once covered and painted they may look like metal. Building those models taught me a lot about aeronautics, knowledge I was later able to apply to the manufacture of real airplanes.

INVADERS
The invasion has begun
Jellyfish Invasion
Day 3

Maria opened the door leading into the conference room, she was wearing orange athletic clothes that matched her hair and the freckles on her cheeks. It was the kind of comfortable clothes she liked to wear, except when she had to give a lecture or present one of her projects to the board of directors. The truth is she was attractive even in fleece pajamas, printed with little sheep. Growing up with four brothers and always wearing pants had not detracted one bit from her feminine appeal. The room was completely dark, you couldn't see a thing. The noise of a chair dragging across the floor came from the back.

"Hello? Is anyone there?" Her voice was clear and without echo, absorbed by the soundproofed walls of the hall.

No one answered, this made her uncomfortable, the darkness frightened her a lot and anything could be found in that place. Maybe there were cockroaches on the floor and walking without light she could step on them, which seemed utterly disgusting to her: "What if there were rats? Maybe the noise from the chair was caused by one of them? But if so, it would have to be a huge rat."

She walked slowly towards the back of the room. Her heart began to beat rapidly. She thought she was doing something stupid. But what the hell was she doing? It would be best to leave that place and return to her room, besides she had a lot of work to do. In complete darkness she turned around heading from memory towards the exit. Again the sound of a chair moving was heard.

"Who's there? Tim? Do you want to stop messing around already?"

At that moment someone turned on the light blinding the doctor, she looked towards the back of the room and saw several human figures.

"What the hell are you doing?"

"Shh! Stop shouting, the whole ship is going to find out." Tim snapped.

They were seated around a table at the back of the room, all set to start the card game.

"What were you doing with the lights off?"

"Can't you see?" Timothy shook his head from side to side in a resigned gesture, however the tone was playful. "This is an underground gambling den, if the captain or any of the officers were to hear about it... Seeing someone open the door, we turned off the light just in case."

At the table there were eight in total, seven men and the doctor, who was the only woman. After an hour of playing she was by far the one who had accumulated the most chips.

"We're in the same boat as always, you're going to pluck us all... I don't understand what you're doing dissecting those disgusting bugs when you could make a professional career out of gambling. A poker player of your level could easily earn several thousand euros a week."

"And what would you do without me?" She winked at him with a smile. "Besides I'm very fond of my work."

"Well, you can tell me why? Always depending on grants, having to convince groups of investors just to barely make ends meet with a measly salary and having to work in miserable conditions."

"Do you think these are miserable conditions?" She raises her chin pointing to what they were doing.

"You know what I'm referring to... the damned years we spent in the tropics, in South America and Africa. I also haven't forgotten the four months we spent in Siberia. Having to go outside to take a crap, with a shovel and toilet paper... I think my ass still hasn't thawed out. "

Dr. Garcia was silent for a moment, then stood up and began to speak as if she were the President of the government. Embers from her past as an environmental activist.

"And doing something for humanity, trying to save this damned planet... friendship and good times?"

Tim's face was very white and he was sweating profusely, small beads of sweat remained adhered to his forehead, spaced a few millimeters apart.

"Are you okay?" Maria asked him.

"Not very well to be honest, I think I've caught a cold, I'd better go to my cabin." - and he left the meeting room staggering.

The ship sailed wrapped in a dense, icy white shroud like snow, following the jellyfish trail on sonar. On the monitors, a river formed by the millions of jellyfish swimming through the ocean glowed phosphorescent green, like columns of legionnaires marching towards Rome.

HIGHLIGHTED NEWS September 1st

All communication lost with the Hesperides

Thanks to a confidential source, a collaborator of this newspaper, we have found out that the Hesperides has gone missing. Both the Spanish government and the Pentagon and UN committee have refused to make statements, it seems everything is being kept top secret. The last transmission from the ship was over twenty four hours ago, since then it has been impossible to contact it. It has disappeared from radar screens and is not responding to any calls. We spoke with Commander Ignacio Martínez, a sailor with over forty years of experience and he told us that in the waters where the Hesperides is sailing, storms are frequent and can indeed interfere with both communications and radar signals.

Apparently there are several ships in the area that have suffered the same mishap, we do not know if there is a connection between them, but information reaches us from the Kremlin about a Russian icebreaker that finds itself in similar circumstances.

We will continue to hope to receive news of the missing ship as soon as possible. From here we wish them luck and hope to be able to rely on the scientific reports from the group led by Dr. Maria Garcia as soon as possible.

Commander Bruce's Flight Logs

The ground was soft, the grass was not tall, it had barely sprouted from the ground and the air was full of the smell of damp earth. It had been raining for several days and the soggy ground had not absorbed all the water. I looked for an open area, a place with no obstacles, at the back of the park, where it became open field. It was a large enough area to perform the first tests.

I left the backpack containing the paragliding wing in the middle of the clearing and watched the sky for a few moments, it was dotted with clouds moving quickly at high altitude. I picked up a few blades of grass in my hand and tossed them high above my head, to get a feel for the wind speed. The thin leaves flew away quickly, it didn't seem like a good day, but I had been waiting a long time for the rain to stop and wanted to finally test the equipment.

For as long as I can remember I have always wanted to fly, to fly like birds do. And I did it in dreams, where I flew flapping my arms as if they were wings. Later, when I was a little older, the experiments came, jumping from any slightly elevated place, with all kinds of contraptions, umbrellas, sheets tied into parachutes, small wings made of wood or cork and even experiments with magic capes, but none of the elements used worked, beyond bruises and bumps. It took many years until I finally saved up enough money to buy a real flying contraption. It was an old paraglider, not used too much, some patches on the sail and a few lines on the right harness changed. For all this, I got it at a good price. The young man who sold it to me, told me that for now he wasn't going to fly, he was expecting his first child, and until he was older, he preferred to keep his feet on the ground. I've heard that many times, argued in a thousand different ways, as if we were really masters of our destiny, if you don't do risky sports it's assumed you'll live to old age. Simplifying things so much leaves me perplexed, over time I've seen people around me die in the most absurd way. A heart attack in a young person, lightning striking the person walking through the mountains under a blue, clear sky. He handed me the paragliding backpack as if it were loaded with explosives. "Go kill yourself if you want, I have a wife and kids."

INVADERS
The invasion has begun
Jellyfish Invasion
Day 4

The captain, a middle-aged man, with very short, curly hair, tall and thin, with a physique similar to that of a marathon runner, was running around the deck of the ship early in the morning. It was part of his regular training, because although he was over fifty he was still in very good physical shape. The fog prevented him from seeing more than a few meters away, he followed the path marked by a red paint line on the floor. The Hesperides by this point in the mission was very far north, with daytime temperatures barely reaching a few degrees above zero on the mercury. That morning he had gone out running in long sweatpants and a gray fleece sweatshirt. The hood gave him a certain pugilistic analogy. He heard footsteps behind him, quick strides approaching him rapidly, he turned to see who it was.

"Doctor! I didn't know you were into athletics. You're in shape." - He greeted her informally given the circumstances.

"I can say the same about the first part, I'm not so sure about the second, I've been having a bad time lately..."

"That happens to all of us, we never see ourselves as good enough, especially in my case, with age starting to take its toll."

"Nonsense, you look like a kid!"

"I appreciate the compliment, especially coming from such a pretty woman."

They kept running side by side, although the pace was a bit fast for the captain, making him pant, while for Maria it was too slow and her legs were starting to freeze.

"Don't worry about me, continue at your own pace..." - He was out of breath.

"I want to tell you something, don't you think this sudden fog is a bit strange, and that we have no news from the weather station?"

"I didn't say anything before so as not to alarm you, but we've been out of communication since last night. We can't get in touch with anyone, the radio doesn't work and the satellite signal is gone and what's worse, we're reaching Arctic waters, where we're supposed to meet the Russian icebreaker Arktika which will clear the way for us."

"I didn't know the Russians were in on this too."

"I see there are many things you are unaware of, unfortunately I can't tell you much since the operation is totally secret. The Russians, the Japanese and even the Americans are suffering from this damned jellyfish plague, what seemed like an isolated episode has become a global crisis."

"Is the UN and NATO involved in this? Don't tell me they want to disguise a military mission as a scientific expedition?"

"I give you my word that I don't know anything else, I've told you all this because I think you are one of the brightest researchers of all time, although I am military I read a lot of scientific articles and am very interested in your work. The nuclear icebreaker Arktika is armed with nuclear warheads, our orders are to wait for you to locate the jellyfish breeding point and provide the coordinates to the Arktika to proceed with cleaning ground zero. "

"But you guys have gone crazy! What do you mean clean? You mean contaminate for centuries with radioactive material one of the purest areas of the planet. Furthermore: How do you know that this will contain the plague? Is there anything else I should know? Does it seem logical to you to use nuclear weapons against a jellyfish shoal?" -

She was furious, she felt like punching whoever ordered such nonsense in the face.

"I give you my word that I don't know anything else, I've told you all this because I think you are one of the brightest researchers of all time, although I am military I read a lot of scientific articles and am very interested in your work. The nuclear icebreaker Arktika is armed with nuclear warheads, our orders are to wait for you to locate the jellyfish breeding point and provide the coordinates to the Arktika to proceed with cleaning ground zero. "

"But you guys have gone crazy! What do you mean clean? You mean contaminate for centuries with radioactive material one of the purest areas of the planet. Furthermore: How do you know that this will contain the plague? Is there anything else I should know? Does it seem logical to you to use nuclear weapons against a jellyfish shoal?" - She was furious, she felt like punching whoever ordered such nonsense in the face.

"I give you my word that I don't know anything else, I've told you all this because I think you are one of the brightest researchers of all time, although I am military I read a lot of scientific articles and am very interested in your work. The nuclear icebreaker Arktika is armed with nuclear warheads, our orders are to wait for you to locate the jellyfish breeding point and provide the coordinates to the Arktika to proceed with cleaning ground zero. "

"I swear I don't know anything else, I've told you all this because I think you're one of the brightest researchers of all time. Even though I'm military, I read a lot of scientific articles and am very interested in your work. If you find a way to solve this without the nuclear bombing taking place, I give you my word that I will personally put you in contact with high command, so you can speak with them."

Commander Bruce's Flight Logs

The same day I bought it, it started raining heavily, so my plan to go to the park and try it out was ruined. The weather dragged on, sitting in my room looking at the paragliding backpack for a while and out the window at the raindrops falling on the glass. The wait was endless. I finally came up with an idea, I would go to the library looking for a book about motorless flight. The municipal library building was huge, huge in empty space, the scarce shelves seemed designed in minimalist fashion. I searched but could only find old books, and I say old not classic. Old books about science and technology, which over time seemed to have been written by comedians: Nuclear power, the energy of the future, and it showed an image on the cover, depicting the city of the future, happy people and children playing in a park next to a nuclear power plant. The best aviation book I found was one with lots of drawings and very large letters in the children's section. I left the building disillusioned, a hollow monument, with which the mayor had surely won the election. I took the train and headed downtown, to one of the largest bookstores. The shelves were full of commercial books, trashy novels about the self-centered millionaire who likes beating women with a whip and falls in love with a young maiden. I also found great collections of esoteric books, explaining that you don't need to diet or exercise to be fit, you also don't need to study to pass an exam, everything can be achieved by wearing the right colored crystal necklace. I asked one of the saleswomen about the recreational aviation books and she told me which section I could find them in. I went down to the basement, where the books I was interested in were, a small shelf with a few volumes mixed together. The same children's tales from the library and some flight manuals written in foreign languages. A small yellow cover book caught my attention, which I thought I read the word paragliding on. Of course, the new generations don't know what I'm talking about, the joy of finally finding the book you're looking for, now with the internet everything is easier, you can find tutorials on anything.

For several days all I did was read and study that small manual, although it was a book with few pages it contained a lot of information. I reviewed it over and over until I memorized it. The new day finally arrived, it dawned cloudy, but without rain, so I got ready to go out and test the paraglider.

Once at the place I thought would be best to deploy it, I observed the wind speed. Although there was a considerable gusty wind, I was very eager to finally spread the sail and didn't pay it much attention. Once deployed on the ground, with the lines and harnesses already hooked to the carabiners, I put on the harness. It was an old model, from the first generations. The pilot's position was seated with the back straight, as if I was on a swing. The air intakes and cells of the sail were large, it was a not very aerodynamic model, a wing with low glide ratio and low cruising speed. Once in the middle and facing the wind, I prepared to lift it up. I was nervous and remembered some of the advice I had read. The sail inflated violently and pulled me so hard it dragged me on my back across the ground. Instead of backing off, which would have been the most reasonable thing, I tried again more vigorously. This time I took off vertically, instead of moving forward and gliding smoothly down the slope, it went straight up at full speed, flying backwards. When I reached about a thousand meters altitude, I stabilized facing the wind, I thought it would be best to turn to be able to descend in a spiral, but with the side wind, the sail folded. I then remembered the section of the manual explaining the procedure to redeploy the paraglider. And the phrase that said: Always face the wind. I thought everything was lost, that I would fly backwards until reaching a height where I could no longer breathe due to lack of oxygen or descend at high speed until getting electrocuted by catching on the power lines. I calmed down and took control of the situation, if I couldn't fly facing forward, I would do it backwards, as if driving a car in reverse. That's how I crossed the mountain range, until the wind subsided and I was able to land in a small clearing in the woods. When I touched ground it kept dragging me until I crashed into an oak tree. I felt like the astronaut returning home and finally setting foot on Earth.

INVADERS
The invasion has begun
Jellyfish Invasion
Day 5

The doctor works against the clock in the lab, they have collected samples from several specimens, but they are unable to decipher what their life cycle is, why they reproduce so quickly, where they come from and why they travel from the pole to our coasts. But what seems even more incomprehensible to her is that the army is behind all this and also wants to carry out a nuclear attack. "Have they all gone crazy? What is behind the proliferation of these animals?"

"Lee, have you seen Tim?" The woman denied distractedly, she was focused on her work.

"I think he's sick, I haven't seen him leave his cabin."

On one of the lab tables there was a stainless steel tray, near a cage with a couple of white mice eating pellets without a care. Dr. Lee Oneal, an African American woman, about fifty years old and over two hundred pounds, approached and stretched her broad, chubby hand to grab the sample.

"It was to be expected, he always gets sick when he travels by boat." - The resigned look.

"I thought he had gotten used to it by now."

"That's what I thought too, plus this time I recommended he take motion sickness pills, but it's the same, he's a hopeless case. Do me a favor... bring me one of the trays with the specimens we collected this morning." - She pointed to the right side of the table where Mrs. Oneal was working.

At that moment, as if some mechanism were activated inside the jellyfish, a small harpoon-shaped appendage fired, like a chameleon's tongue.

"Oh my God!" - She jumped back, standing up, looking at the tray with her eyes so wide they nearly popped out of their sockets.

"What's going on?" Dr. Maria Garcia was frightened by the woman's sudden reaction.

"Look, look! Do you see it?" The huge woman shouted in fear.

Maria approached quickly, she was totally amazed, she couldn't believe what she was seeing. The jellyfish attacked ferociously, launching its strange appendage and injecting its venom into the poor little mouse. It had suddenly activated, emerging from its lethargy upon sensing the warm body of the small rodent.

"What a curious specimen, it resembles the marine snails of the family Cónidae. Conus geographus, Conus aulicus, Conus textile... which have a gland connected to a harpoon-shaped radula tooth that they launch at their prey, injecting them with a very potent venom."

The little mouse soon fell paralyzed to the floor, it began to breathe rapidly, choking, while the jellyfish began covering part of its body. Then the connection broke, the thin filamentous tentacle, glassy in appearance, snapped and the jellyfish which until that moment had not stopped moving in the water of the tray, became paralyzed. Dr. Lee approached cautiously, her hands covered with thick gloves normally used when working with chemicals. She wielded a scalpel in her right hand and at the speed of a Japanese chef sliced the animal into thin sushi slices. There was no movement, the jellyfish had already died when the appendage separated from its body. The viscous mass that remained adhered to the small mammal seemed to pulse, then it began to move and introduced itself into the animal's body, entering through its nose.

"Look, look doctor, it seems to be moving now."

"What the hell!"

The rodent got back on its feet, as if nothing had happened, and the first thing it did was go to another of the specimens it shared the cage with. It cornered it in a corner and attacked it, biting it on the back, the victim wanted to break free, it wouldn't stop screaming in pain, when it managed to break free it had a greenish secretion on the bite wound, and in little time it went through the same process as its companion.

"It seems like some kind of virus, with behavior similar to rabies, but with an incredible speed of spreading." - Dr. Maria Garcia, while maintaining her composure, showed a dreadful attitude in her expressions. "We have to take extreme precautions, we will have to quarantine the lab and all personnel who have handled these creatures."

Commander Bruce's Flight Logs

If someone ever asked me for proof to show them they are alive, I would take them flying in my plane, skimming the ground over endless crop fields. Flying over the tall cornfields, over the undulating wheat and rye crops. Feeling the wind on your face at sunset and the vivid smell of vegetation. At sunset there is a magical moment, a moment when time seems to stand still. The sun descends over the horizon and a soft breeze blows, forming waves over the cereal fields that seem liquid like the sea. When the sun disappears below the horizon and the skies become multicolored, at that precise instant when day gives way to night, the breeze suddenly stops and everything becomes calm. The clouds in the sky like Venus's long, thin fingers take on different textures and hues. The tenuous atmosphere allows the small pollen grains to rise into the stratosphere. White dandelions floating like snowflakes.

INVADERS
The invasion has begun
Jellyfish Invasion
Day 6

Dr. Maria Garcia walked down the narrow hallway to Timothy's cabin door. She knocked softly:

"Knock, knock..." - She made two quick series of knocks on the cabin door.

"Tim how are you feeling? Are you any better?"

She waited a few seconds, but no one answered. An intense silence could be heard accompanied by the incessant background noise produced by the Hesperides' diesel engines. She waited again before knocking. It was quite cold in the hallway, it seemed like the heating wasn't working at full capacity. The frosted glass ceiling lights with steel and brass guards dimmed their glow. For a second everything went dark. Dr. Maria was starting to suspect something was not right on the ship, she had to speak to the captain as soon as possible.

"Knock, knock, knock..." - This time she pounded on the door forcefully. "Tim, let me in, I want to examine you."

She placed her right hand on the doorknob and it opened, the hinges creaked emitting an unpleasant sound that made her hair stand on end. The cabin was dark, she felt around for the light switch, sliding her hand along the rough wall, over the several layers of paint covering the steel, until she found it. The light came on slowly, the low consumption bulbs in the rooms took a while to warm up and illuminate at full power. She looked around: Everything was thrown on the floor, there were books, clothes, papers everywhere, it looked like a hurricane had gone through. On the bed, under the sheets was a huge lump in human form.

"Tim, are you there? Are you okay?" Once again only the disconcerting silence accompanied by the background noise from the engine room could be heard.

Maria grabbed the sheet by one end and with a quick jerk uncovered the mattress. On the bed there was a greenish mass, the smell was nauseating, she had to cover her nose with her hand. It was an organic, putrid fluid similar to what came out of the infected mouse in the lab. The sound of a footstep startled her, putting her on alert. Out of the corner of her eye, before she could turn to clearly see what it was, she sensed a human figure entering through the door. It was a bulky figure, of a tall, strong man like Timothy. Before she could turn her head to look at him straight on, she felt him lunge at her. Thanks to adrenaline and years of physical training, she jumped back and managed to get away without him laying a hand on her. The man lost his balance and rolled onto the floor. Now she could see her attacker better, she looked at him for a split second as she ran to the door. With his back to her, face against the floor she couldn't recognize him, but by his body and clothes she was sure it was the Englishman. Then he turned around and she was able to contemplate his face, or what was left of it, as parts of his flesh were missing and his nose was practically nonexistent, it looked like he had been burned with acid. When he fell to the floor he had hit his head on the metal bed frame, causing a gash on his forehead. The cut was very deep, slicing through muscle and bone, but there was absolutely no blood, instead a gelatinous greenish drool oozed from the inside.

"Tim, is that you? Tim, what's wrong with you?" - The only response was a growl more characteristic of an animal than a person.

Without a word he lunged at her again, but this time she was prepared and ran out of the cabin. She raced down the hallway at full speed, trying to leave her pursuer behind. The long, narrow hallway curved to the left at the end to finally end at a small staircase leading up. She jumped onto the third step and grabbed the metal railing, climbed the stairs as fast as she could, although she couldn't help but stumble. Just a few millimeters prevented her face from hitting the floor, she had held tightly to the railing saving her from the blow. She had the rectangular hatch giving access to the upper level right in front of her. When she already had half her body out and her pulse was returning to normal, a hand grabbed her firmly by the ankle.

HIGHLIGHTED NEWS September 5th
Riots multiply throughout the city

A wave of unprecedented crime is ravaging cities, our bureaus in different parts of the planet report that these are not isolated events. No matter where in the world, the culture, race or religion, a violent anarchy has been unleashed everywhere. We do not know what motivates these people, some sociologists point to radical groups that have grown due to the enormous economic crisis we have been suffering for several years. Certainly these arguments do not seem to make sense, there are doctors who associate this attitude with some kind of virus similar to rabies, which is still completely unknown.

From the window of our office we can see the maddened crowd running through the streets. Disturbances continue along 33rd Street. A group of bloodied people from the brawls are running towards our building...

Reporting from Mexico City is Eulalio Santos, yours truly, who will keep you informed.

"Stop transmitting Eulalio and run, help me! We have to barricade this door, we can't let them in!" - The camera rolled across the floor losing the image, but the audio kept transmitting.

"Oh my God!"

Commander Bruce's Flight Logs

The work shift rotated every week, seven consecutive days of work followed by five days off. The forest covered a huge expanse that stretched to infinity through the wildlands of northern Canada and Alaska. The only way to reach some areas was by taking off from provisional airfields that were only used during peak fire risk seasons. They had a wooden cabin where they rested when on duty. At the emergency stations, lost in the depths of the forests, three people lived together, Commander, co-pilot and radio operator. Pilot and co-pilot had to have mechanical knowledge, to always keep the aircraft ready. The interior of the cabin was cozy, as long as the radio operator left his boots outside. It would be a perfect place if they had installed individual beds instead of bunk beds. In any case, no one complained when they got the bed after a long day's work in the forest. The radio was on a table by the window, so the operator could work while gazing at the immense landscape. Peter the radio operator had gained the trust of a squirrel, he fed it every day, and over time he left the window ajar and the little animal came in every morning to ask for its ration of nuts. On stormy days, which were quite common in midsummer, I liked to spend them sitting in one of the comfortable armchairs reading a book. We had a shelf full of books and board games; in the pre-internet era this was the best entertainment. Lucas, the co-pilot had decorated the wooden walls of the cabin with antique mountaineering objects: an ice axe, crampons, rope, carabiners, wedges and pitons, giving the interior a certain alpine museum flair.

INVADERS
The invasion has begun
Jellyfish Invasion
Day 7

Researcher Lee Oneal ran down the hallway towards the lab, by the marked expression on her face and nervous look, it was clear she had realized something was not right on the Hesperides. Her face showed no fear or terror, rather indignation, she seemed irritated. The stout woman strode with determination, very clear about what she had to do. About twenty meters ahead was a wheeled table, like those used in hotels to take dinner to the rooms, but instead of carrying food, its large steel tray was full of needles for taking samples in the lab. A door opened and out came a soldier with his uniform torn to shreds, jaw unhinged, growling like a dog. The table with the lab tools was in the middle. Mrs. Lee was not scared, she took a deep breath and quickened her pace, rushing to meet the infected soldier. She was like a freight train at full speed, like an enraged bull. She got to the wheeled table. Without a word Dr. Oneal grabbed the tray with both hands and smashed it in his face. The infected being immediately stopped growling, collapsed from the huge blow and fell to the floor with needles all over his face. She had left his face ready to win the Guinness World Record for most facial piercings. She moved on to the lab and once inside pressed the red emergency button that automatically sealed and locked the premises.

DR. MARIA GARCIA FOUGHT to free herself from her colleague Tim. The truth is he no longer seemed to be her colleague, neither physically nor mentally, that furious thing, straight out of one of Stephen King's worst nightmares, held her firmly by the ankle and tried to bite her. Every time his mouth got close to the doctor's leg she kicked him hard, knocking out several of his teeth. At the rate they were flying, the infected man was going to need dentures to be able to bite his victims. While there is no doubt that the doctor was in great shape, she was still human and her strength was starting to fade. Her heart was racing, her erratic breathing wasn't enough and she felt she was going to faint at any moment. But she would not give up easily, as long as she had an ounce of energy left she would keep kicking wildly. That damned demon pulled harder and harder and the exit hatch seemed farther away by the moment. When she thought all was lost, hands grabbed her by the arms and pulled her. She jumped through the metal door giving access to the upper level and immediately the solid steel door closed.

What the hell is going on? Most of my crew has gone crazy! - shouted the captain shaking the doctor by the arms to bring her back to her senses.

It took her a few seconds to react, she couldn't get the image of Tim making noises like a beast and spitting foam from his mouth out of her head.

We have to get to the lab.

I think it's safer if we stay here, out there everyone has gone crazy.

We can't waste any more time, I need to do some tests in the lab, we have to find a way to solve what's happening. We need to keep studying those specimens.

One way or another the breeding zone will be destroyed in a matter of hours. There are eighteen hours left for the Artika to proceed with the launch.

These words further disturbed Maria, she was not at all sure this was the solution, the only thing that seemed certain in all this was that the military commanders seemed to know something. Had these strange jellyfish come from some military lab where biological weapons were produced? Perhaps genetically modified animals inoculated with some kind of rabies-like virus? She needed to do more tests, it was paramount to know how radiation would affect these animals...

Emergency Broadcast

All radio and television channels broadcast the same message over and over:

A curfew is declared, the army is in charge of your security. Do not leave your homes, close doors and windows. Remain on standby for further orders. Anyone on the streets will be seen as a potential risk, state security forces will act accordingly.

Remember to stay in your homes, do not open the door to anyone, be alert for new orders.

Individuals who disobey orders will be treated as high risk.

The broadcast was repeated over and over, while screams, crashes of vehicles and bursts of automatic weapons fire could be heard in the streets, like military rifles and machine guns.

Commander Bruce's Flight Logs

The Canadair CL-215 amphibious twin engine aircraft rested at the head of the grass runway, next to the side of the house. The runway was long enough for the plane to be able to take off and land safely, although the width was quite tight. A clearing in the forest surrounded by crowded trees. If there was no fire, the plane remained on the ground, routine engine checks were performed starting up its radial engines. Smaller, faster planes that took off from bases near large cities did reconnaissance flights. Waiting on the ground unable to fly became tedious and boring for Bruce.

The legendary Canadair CL-215 seaplane looked like it came from a museum, it was one of the first models without turbocharged engines. Although the ground crew were always happy to hear the guttural sound emitted by its engines, especially under adverse circumstances, when the seaplanes were the only ones that could face the flames. It was a slow plane, about four hundred kilometers maximum speed, but it had a wide range. It could carry over five thousand liters of water. A quick pass over the surface of any of the nearby lakes and its tank was full. The urban legend of the frogman who was diving in a swamp and ended up dumped by a seaplane on the pines is a myth, the charging ports are very small, the plane passes over the surface at high speed and pressure does the rest.

INVADERS
The invasion has begun
Jellyfish Invasion
Day 8

For several hours there were shouts and growls, then silence fell. Dr. Maria Garcia knew she could not stay locked in her cabin for long. She had no water or food, plus the door was very flimsy and if they found her they would break it down by force. The only way to stop this was to get to the lab to do more testing. She carefully opened the door making no noise and went out into the hallway armed with a mop handle. She couldn't find anything else on the ship that could be used as a defensive weapon. Everything was welded, attached to the floor or metal walls. Despite appearances the sharpened end and length of the slat made it a good defense, she could lash out with the tip and keep anyone who tried to get too close at a distance. The hallway lights failed continuously, dimming almost to the point of going out for a few seconds. It seemed something was breaking down in the engine room. She walked slowly leaning against one of the walls of the corridor, attentive to the end where there was an intersection of hallways. The light bulbs suddenly increased in intensity, the bright almost blinding light revealed blood stained white walls everywhere. Maria panicked, which increased when she heard footsteps approaching the hallway intersection. She gripped the pole tightly preparing for anything. She saw a wavering human shadow moving from side to side, just as it reached the intersection, the light dimmed almost to the point of going out completely. She stood silent leaning against the wall and watched as the figure of a man, with a kitchen knife stuck in his back, dragged one leg as he walked, violently jerking his head. He looked at her for an instant, but did not detect her, he sniffed twice, in the same way an animal would, then continued to the left, leaving the path on the right clear. She breathed again and prepared to face the final stretch, she knew the lab was just a few meters away. In the gloom she walked slowly and carefully making no noise, so unlucky that she bumped the fire extinguisher hanging on the wall with her shoulder, it came off the wall and rolled thunderously on the floor. The doctor didn't think twice, she ran, she knew it was her only chance to reach the lab alive. As she took the right hallway, she caught a glimpse of a group of several infected people running towards her from the opposite corridor, among them was the one with the knife stuck in his back. She ran with all her might, she had a bit of a head start when she reached the bulletproof glass door of the lab. She quickly swiped her ID card over the electronic lock but the doors did not open.

"Help!" - She cried out in desperation.

Then Dr. Lee Oneal appeared on the other side and pressing the emergency button, the doors unlocked and Maria was able to get in just before the group of infected people reached her. Once the doors were sealed again, her heart rate returned to normal. On the other side of the thick glass, the infected moved back and forth, guided by hearing and smell, they did not seem to see very well.

"What the hell is going on?" Dr. Lee Oneal looked exhausted. "Have they all gone crazy?"

"I don't know. I think it's some kind of viral disease transmitted by jellyfish, similar to rabies."

"Yes, I've seen them get sick first, run a high fever for a few hours and later go crazy and homicidally attack everyone."

"I think that's why the disease has spread so quickly." Now as if her strength was leaving her, Maria collapsed, she sat on the floor with her face on her knees crying. "I had to kill Dr. Timothy."

"That was no longer Tim, whatever it was it was no longer human, you did what you had to do to survive. At least the emergency generator works here, we have light, water, coffee and salty snacks I managed to get from the vending machine in the hallway."

"Have you tried to communicate with the outside?" - She asked still teary-eyed.

"I've tried it every way, but the lab computers' wifi depends on outside power, without an antenna it doesn't work."

The priority was to establish communication. The Russian icebreaker Artika was just a few miles away.

Commander Bruce's Flight Logs

Bruce was a young man, with a charismatic smile, all the men greeted him and all the women smiled back. Such was his composure and the way he carried himself that any co-pilot who had flown with him would trust him with his life. He was tall and handsome, though he didn't leave it all to genetics, to stay in shape and be able to do his job, he ran ten kilometers every morning. He had a well-defined chin and jawline, his lips were thick and his mouth wide, fine wrinkles formed at the corners of his eyes when he smiled. He had an expressive face that evoked a sense of familiarity in everyone. He had tranquil, calm blue-gray eyes that could be penetrating when he wanted them to be. His very short hair was dark in winter and lightened as it grew and the sun bleached it in summer. The classic style, he had been getting his hair cut at the same old barbershop since he was a boy. Fabian the barber was retired, but he lived next to the shop and it was enough to ring the bell for him to come down and fix Bruce's hair in five minutes. He wore jeans all year round, accompanied by pure wool sweaters in winter. He always wore an old brown leather aviator jacket. He liked antiques related to aviation and he had won that jacket many years earlier playing poker in the canteen of the airfield where he worked as a mechanic before getting his pilot's license.

INVADERS
The invasion has begun
Jellyfish Invasion
Day 9

Dr. Lee Oneal performed tests on the infected mice to see if she could make a vaccine. Meanwhile, Dr. Maria Garcia worked at a table with an assortment of electronic components. She had dismantled a blender from the lab and removed the electric motor. She pulled out the copper wire from the coil and then wound it around a pencil. With the jack plug from a pair of headphones and a paperclip as a dial, she connected it to the laptop's microphone. She turned the speakers up to full volume. At first there was only background noise, but as she slid the paperclip over the copper coil, suddenly something could be heard. She carefully repositioned the paperclip on the spot and this time she heard a man's voice giving instructions in Russian. At the end of the message it repeated, this time in English. It was a transmission from the Artika.

Artika emergency transmission

"What are they talking about, what do they mean proceed with the launch?" - Asked Dr. Oneal.

"The Russian icebreaker is armed with nuclear missiles, after losing communication with high command for a long period of time, they have orders to launch the missiles at the target."

"But that would be disastrous..." - The woman said very worried.

"Disastrous?"

"Yes, all the tests I've done show that jellyfish have increased growth when exposed to radiation."

To save the human species, they would have to prevent the missile launch at all costs. They had no way to communicate with the Russian ship. So they prepared as best they could with everything they had on hand in the lab, put on thick NBQ suits, including helmets, and reinforced arms and legs with duct tape to prevent infected bites from penetrating them. They armed themselves with spears tipped with sharp scalpel blades.

They prepared for a moment before opening the door and leaving, you had to be focused and calm. Now the central hallway was dark and nothing could be seen. Mrs. Lee carried a small flashlight and Maria had a fluorescent gel bar, which emitted a yellowish-green chemical glow.

"I don't think they see very well, if we don't make noise they may not detect us." - Maria warned before Oneal pressed the emergency button that opened the door.

They moved slowly and cautiously down the central corridor without encountering any of them until they reached the hallway intersection. Before turning towards the exit, they heard asthmatic breathing and growling.

"Turn off the flashlight and don't leave my side." - She held the chemical glow stick in her hand, its dim glow did not attract the attention of the group of infected people.

They sneaked very slowly, leaning against the wall. One of the soldiers missing his right cheekbone, as if it had been ripped off in one bite, began to move restlessly, as if sensing the presence of the doctors, turning back and forth, growling and sniffing. He couldn't see them, apparently they were practically blind and were guided mainly by smell and hearing. Perhaps he noticed the strange smell of the polypropylene suits and butyl gloves. Maria Garcia raised her right leg to take a step forward, but at that moment Lee stopped her by grabbing her forcefully by the arm. She signaled for her to look at the floor. There was broken glass, if the restless infected soldier who was just five meters from them had heard it, he would have detected them. She put her foot on the clean floor and they continued forward until they managed to get out of the hallway intersection. From there the area was clear and in a short time they managed to get up on deck. The fog was less dense and from the starboard railing they could see the silhouette of the Artika like a dark shadow. It was anchored a few hundred meters away. They lowered the Zodiac used for surveys and collecting samples. They climbed down the ladder and to avoid attracting attention they used the oars instead of starting the outboard motor.

Commander Bruce's Flight Logs

Fire is pure energy, you can feel its heat, its energy from a distance. Fire is a living being, a being that feeds on everything in its path. We have coexisted with it since the dawn of humanity, it still impresses us today as much as it did the first day and we can't take our eyes off the flames. It fascinates and attracts us. We try to understand it, handle it and manipulate it, but we never succeed. It always escapes our control. Primitive men made a deal, they came to an agreement with the god of fire, a delicate, difficult to understand agreement. A pact with the devil that has lasted to this day, that has allowed us to dominate the planet. An agreement with the devil that we have forgotten and that comes every now and then to take what we hold most dear. The heat reaches you like the desert sun, forcefully, hitting your face. Fire is always on a war footing, fighting it is an all out battle. Pilots had to learn to read it, to understand how it reacts and thinks. You should never lose respect for it. You should never declare war on it.

We stayed up all night, waiting for the first light of dawn. Throughout the night, reports kept coming in on the radio about fires spreading through the forest. The storm lasted all night, an electrical storm that barely dropped four raindrops. Lightning kept lighting up the sky, the electrical discharges overlapped each other and the thunderous sound resembled explosions from an engine. The three of us remained alert by the radio, the operator, the co-pilot and me, waiting to be given the order to leave. During the night a large number of personnel had been deployed, the ground crews were unable to contain the flames. The different hotspots fueled by strong winds were spreading uncontrolled. Hardly anyone has ever seen the true power of fire, what it is capable of when conditions allow it. When fuel and air join forces it becomes a diabolical monster, impossible to contain. It creates its own wind, the devil's breath, it can uproot trees and transport them burning several kilometers away, opening new hotspots in different parts of the forest. Some, like eucalyptus loaded with resins and combustible oils, explode like gunpowder barrels.

INVADERS
The invasion has begun
Jellyfish Invasion
Day 10

Dr. Maria Garcia's silicone sports watch marked exactly midnight, it also indicated that her pulse was slightly elevated and that she had walked over five thousand steps in the last twelve hours. She was on the deck of the Artika, enveloped in dense fog. They headed for the bridge, the ship seemed deserted, as if the entire crew had jumped overboard. All the lifeboats were gone. In the cold temperatures, the rubber suits lost flexibility and both women had difficulty walking. On the hatch-shaped door giving access inside, they saw the first blood stains, confirming that the Russian icebreaker had suffered the same fate as the Hesperides.

They followed the arrows painted on the walls that supposedly indicated the direction to the bridge, since everything appeared written in Cyrillic and was almost impossible to decipher. The access door was locked from the inside, they banged on it with a fire extinguisher until they heard voices inside.

"Open the door, we're from the Hesperides." - shouted Dr. Garcia.

Instantly they heard the door lock mechanism turning and the door opened. Inside there were only two young men, a sergeant and a badly wounded soldier, he had a broken leg. He must have gotten it in a fall while fleeing, otherwise he would have already turned into one of the infected. The sergeant's expression changed immediately when he realized there was no rescue team, only the two doctors. Before he could close the door, an avalanche of infected people rushed in from the hallway. Dr. Lee Oneal had already taken off the helmet of her NBQ suit when she was knocked to the ground with a shove. The helmet rolled across the floor as she struggled to get a Russian soldier off of her. She was a strong woman and with a sweep of her hand managed to push him away, she crawled on the floor to grab the full helmet, more resembling an astronaut's than a motorcyclist's, with a special carbon filter in the chin area. Maria ran around the control room, trying to leave a couple of infected people behind while looking for the launch console. There was nothing left to do for the two soldiers who had survived locked in the bridge. For a long time the screams of pain from the soldier with the broken leg could be heard, the sergeant didn't even have time to open his mouth, as soon as they came in they pounced on him and killed him with one bite to the jugular. She finally found the panel, with two keys inserted in the locks and a central red button. There were flashing illuminated Cyrillic words. You could also see the countdown, there were only two minutes left for launch. Without having any idea what the Russian symbols meant, she pressed the red button. The countdown stopped immediately and before she could remove the keys, one of the infected bit her on the arm. Dr. Oneal looked like an American football player, four soldiers on top of her trying to eat her, but she pushed them off. Maria Garcia reacted and realizing the teeth had not penetrated the suit, used her scalpel tipped spear. It entered through the infected man's left ear who kept biting her arm and came out the other side. An effective brain wash. She finally pulled out the keys, a few minutes later the result was a pile of corpses riddled with sharp spears and blood splatters reaching the ceiling. The two women had managed to stop eight infected people. But they had to get out of there as soon as possible, the Artika's crew was extensive and there could be hundreds of infected people. They returned via the hallways until they reached the deck. When Maria was about to get into the Zodiac boat, when she looked at Dr. Lee Oneal, she realized something was wrong. And when she got down, when she was in the boat waiting for Oneal to come down, she threw the ladder into the sea, staying on the deck of the Russian icebreaker. Before saying goodbye she turned so Maria could see they had broken her suit and wounded her in the left side. She knew she was infected so she waved goodbye to Maria.

Commander Bruce's Flight Logs

On the ground the firefighters tried to buy time from the fire, cutting off its path before it reached their positions, but the strength of the wind made it impossible to contain. It advanced at an incredible speed. The trees flew overhead in flames like rockets, falling behind their lines. Before they knew it they were trapped between two fronts. The situation took a complete turn, now the priority was not to contain it, they were trying to get out of there by any means. They grouped together in one area, where they tried to resist. The situation was worsening by the moment. They looked for an escape route from the flames, but the heavy smoke made it impossible to see anything. The air burned in their lungs with each breath and the smoke suffocated them. Upon hearing on the radio what was happening, Bruce made the risky decision to take off before dawn. The Canadair CL-215 was not equipped with instrumentation for night navigation. It was like driving a car without lights, running through the woods blindfolded. He could not stand idly by listening as those men perished in the flames. With the headlights of the SUV they lit up the end of the runway.

Bruce quickly climbed into the twin engine plane, while checking the fuel load the co-pilot removed the chocks from the wheels to allow the plane to move. When it was free he rushed up into the seaplane, the pilot pressed the start button and simultaneously both engines began to roar. At the start of the takeoff run the first complications arose. The runway was narrow and with strong wind they needed to turn to face it. The space was too tight to be able to do it, they would need to be towed by the SUV to get into position. That maneuver would take them a long time, time they didn't have. The grass was wet and this gave Bruce an idea. He accelerated to the end of the runway, he was going too fast to be able to stop the plane. The copilot held on tight to his seat. Then he fully pressed the left rudder pedal, pushing it with all his might and only applied the left wheel brake, leaving the right brake off, at that moment the twin engine began to skid on the runway, he cut power to the left engine and pushed the throttle all the way forward on the right one. The Canadair spun around, drifting in a maneuver similar to those performed by Formula 1 drivers when they get sideways off the track going the wrong way. He stopped it in the middle of the runway, perfectly aligned. Now they were upwind, with the wooden cabin and SUV in front of them at the end of the field. He cut power for an instant and reached into his pocket taking out a strip of gum that he popped whole into his mouth. Then he throttled up intermittently, making the engines roar loudly to expel any carbon buildup in the exhaust manifolds. The vehicle's lights marked the end of the runway. The plane started taxiing but couldn't get enough speed to take off, the ground sloped uphill in that direction. If they couldn't get airborne they would crash into the wooden house. Bruce pulled hard on the controls but the plane wouldn't lift off. The distance was shrinking rapidly. Then he pushed the controls down, slightly raising the tail of the plane relieving weight from the wheels.

"You've got control!" - He ordered. The copilot immediately followed the orders.

"Now!" - Bruce shouted and the two men pulled with all their might on the control sticks and the plane finally took off.

The radio operator who was on the ground watching everything saw the plane barreling towards him at full speed. He ran to get off the runway until his legs couldn't go any further, then he dove flat on the ground and felt the air from the propellers and roar of the engines very close to his head. As it passed overhead the man covered himself with his arms and as soon as he heard the noise moving away, he rolled over and saw the plane approaching the wooden house at great speed. The seaplane buzzed the roof of the house, so close that it bent the radio antenna. The radio operator jumped up from the ground and grabbed his cap, waving it in his hand while shouting for joy watching the plane disappear into the darkness.

54

INVADERS
The invasion has begun
Jellyfish Invasion
Morning of Day 16

I've been barricaded in my apartment for two weeks. I had the right idea storing up water, on the fourth day the power supply failed and I was left in darkness, on the fifth the water was cut off. I've lasted all this time with doors and windows closed, watching through a hole in the blinds what was happening outside. The brawls intensified, I saw a lot of violence, assaults, fights to the death, with knives, sticks and teeth. There was a lot of bloodshed. Fires followed from wrecked vehicles and also some homes, which spread from floor to floor and block to block ravaging large areas of the city. Fortunately, my block is separated from the rest in the front by a wide street and in the back by a small park. I've survived all this time hidden without making the slightest noise. It's been three days since anyone's been seen on the street, everything seems deserted. I've waited as long as possible, but I need to go down for supplies.

The elevators weren't working so I had to take the stairs. Between the floor and the wall of the small landing, there were small skylight windows. The lighting was very dim, as some neighbors had bricked up the windows overlooking their terraces. Some floors were completely dark. Most of the apartments had their doors wide open, surely their occupants had run out into the street for help and never returned. I went down the first flight of stairs, luckily this area was well lit. There was shattered glass and objects strewn on the floor: Broken dishes, cutlery and a kitchen knife stained with a brown crust, next to it was a teddy bear. When I looked up at the walls in perspective I noticed more stains of that dark color, shapes of hands and fingers dragging along the walls, then I realized it was coagulated blood. I was tense and clenching my jaw without realizing it out of fear. Panic gradually took over me as I went down the stairs and the darkness intensified, to the point that I couldn't see anything at all. I went down clinging tightly to the railing, stumbling over and over again on things or objects on the floor, some were solid and light, others were soft and heavy. My heart was racing imagining I could be stepping on corpses. I kicked something metallic that rolled down the stairs making a loud crash. If there was anyone nearby they surely would have heard it. I felt someone's presence in the darkness. I thought one of the infected might be lurking, so I ran in terror, crashing into things a thousand times, until I reached the entrance hall. The glass door was broken but it was solid iron-forged and still closed. When I stopped, I realized no one was following me, I calmed myself by breathing deep and slow, then I looked between the bars without sticking my head outside. Everything remained calm, there was absolute silence, nothing could be heard, the whole city seemed motionless like a photograph. There was no movement or sounds, not even from pigeons or sparrows. Absolute calm after a nuclear catastrophe. The ghost town of Pripyat near Chernobyl.

The small shopping center was across the street, about a hundred meters away. I focused on my goal, to cross the deserted streets as quickly as possible, exposing myself for as little time as possible to being seen. I planned an imaginary route in my head, along the most sheltered side of the avenue, passing behind parked cars and the charred structure of a bus lying across the road, then I would cross through the hedges of a small garden and from there go straight to the store entrance.

Three quick breaths and I ran out, once again I noticed the dry blood stains that appeared everywhere, on the metal and windows of the cars. On the ground were dried puddles of the same brownish color. What was disconcerting was the lack of corpses. The scene of the war, the conflict zone itself, the material destruction, burnt out cars and apartments, blood splattered everywhere and absolute silence.

INVADERS
The invasion has begun
Jellyfish Invasion
Afternoon shopping on Day 16

Everything seemed calm in the small shopping mall, some carts loaded with products were queued up waiting their turn behind the registers. It was as if people had evaporated, disintegrated without a trace. If I hadn't seen what happened from the window of my house, the scene wouldn't make any sense. I grabbed a cart and headed for the grocery area. As I got closer the stench of rot intensified, the fresh food, meat and fish had spoiled. In the frozen section the situation was similar, the refrigerated chambers shut off due to lack of power had ruined everything. So I moved to the back, where the canned goods were. Out of habit I started by looking at what was on sale, I immediately realized there was no one to pay, so I loaded the cart with the most expensive products, the finest gourmet foods, five kilos of the most expensive boneless ham, the best candies and chocolates. Then I crossed the central aisle to the electronics section. Batteries, flashlights and also the best Smartphone in the display, the coolest tablet and most powerful laptop. There was no phone signal or internet, but I couldn't resist taking the best products for free. I added two walkie-talkies to the cart, a roll of antenna wire, soldering iron and solder. Then I got the idea to look for a gasoline powered electric generator in the hardware section. They had very small ones, the size of a briefcase. The problem was getting fuel, I couldn't cross half the city to go to the gas station. I thought about the option of siphoning gasoline from the tank of one of the cars on the street with a hose, but they were all wrecked and completely charred. In the chemical section I found alcohol and paint thinner, both highly flammable products that when properly mixed could run the generator. Now that the electricity problem seemed solved and since the situation could drag on indefinitely, I went over to the toy section, grabbed the best video game console and the latest video games, Blu-ray movies and of course the best novels bound in deluxe editions. In total the value of what I had loaded in the cart could easily exceed ten thousand euros. Now my problem was how to get back home with so much stuff, the metal shopping cart had wheels that were too small, plus it made a lot of noise rolling on the sidewalk. In the camping section I loaded everything into a backpack and a mountain bike equipped with saddlebags.

Commander Bruce's Flight Logs

Bruce knew they had only just begun, now the most difficult part remained, to load water into the tanks without crashing. Making a low pass over the lake surface almost in the dark was going to be very tricky. Finding and getting to the lake was simple. The sky cleared and the distant light of the stars and also the orange glow of the fire was reflected on the water. The pilot brought the plane down carefully, slowly, before finally skimming the surface. Despite the gentle touch on the controls, the aircraft hit the water hard and bounced like a stone. Once first contact was made, they had the information needed to make the low pass at the right altitude. While Bruce gently held the aircraft, the copilot remained attentive to the needle on the tank gauges.

"Load complete." - He confirmed with a thumbs up.

The commander pulled on the controls causing the Canadair to climb gaining altitude, then he banked taking a course towards the fire. They skirted the mountain range that began on the north shore and followed it guided by the fire's flashes. Now they were close and could pick up the firefighters' radio transmissions on the ground. Bruce tried to find a place to make a corridor through which they could escape from hell. The virulence of the flames was terrifying, such was the energy it created enormous turbulence causing the heavy seaplane to shudder like a leaf. The ascending columns of hot air shook the aircraft's structure, creaking and cracking continuously. Typical moans and creaks of an old woman. They managed to fly over the flames and entered the middle of the ring of fire where the firefighters were. In the southern area, there was still a small space where the fire was not too violent. Through there perhaps they could get out. He communicated it by radio and the firefighters began walking in that direction, while the plane continued circling over their heads. But the tired, smoke-choked men, some injured trying to escape, advanced too slowly. From the plane the co-pilot tried to stay calm, but from the air they saw they weren't going to make it. The situation was becoming desperate, he could only watch and try to encourage the men to walk faster, but it was useless.

Under the intense heat the human body reaches a point where it starts to fail, the skin dries from lack of sweat. Burning clothes stick to the body like an iron. There comes a point when people give up and curl up on the ground waiting for the end. But these were not ordinary people, they were forest firefighters and they would keep going no matter what. When they finally reached the area where they should escape, the situation had worsened, the flames had moved ahead of them, the evil mind of the fire wanted to take the souls of those men.

The co-pilot ordered them by radio to retreat and regroup in the center. Bruce made a new low pass, looking for a place they could escape through, now the circle had closed and there was no way out. A dog that doesn't want to let go of the bone. Wood and wind, fuel with the perfect mixture of oxygen.

The firefighters managed to fall back to the only area still intact. They could barely breathe the scalding air that burned their lungs. They covered their faces as best they could. Some of the men knelt on the ground praying to God. Their last hope vanished when they saw the seaplane move away gaining altitude.

"Tell the men to cover themselves as best they can." - Bruce's voice remained calm.

He dove straight at the flames, he had to get through them as fast as possible. The old Canadair seemed about to break apart. The engines roared at full power and the aircraft looked like a flaming bird. If they released the water at too high an altitude, it wouldn't even touch the ground, evaporating in the air. They managed to cross the fire and released the load just above the men's heads. Under any other circumstance, it would never have occurred to him to perform such a maneuver, the force of the water could cause serious injury, but at that moment it was the least of his worries. The immense downpour refreshed the men, who for a short period of time felt relieved. Bruce knew it was just a band-aid, the water would soon be consumed. At least this way they bought some time. They climbed again and headed to the lake, now the purplish lights and the different degraded shades of blue painted the sky at dawn. They quickly loaded the tanks and began climbing. One of the old engines began losing power belching black smoke. Bruce reduced power a bit.

"Come on baby, hold on a little longer..." - He gently stroked the control panel.

The engine recovered and they returned to the fire. Now with the first light of day they could see better. The co-pilot ordered them to move north. They descended sharply again not knowing if the old plane could withstand the punishment once more. The co-pilot was heard begging God to save the young firefighters' lives. They shot through the flames at full speed, just as the sun peeked over the mountains. As if by magic or a true miracle, the wind suddenly stopped. The flames diminished and Bruce released all the water at the base of the fire, at the exact point to open a gap. The men on the ground shouted for joy when they saw the corridor in front of them. The co-pilot gave thanks and let out a laugh of joy, but immediately seeing how serious Bruce was, he realized something was wrong.

"This is as far as we go buddy." - He said winking at him.

The huge radial engine on the right wing was on fire, belching gray smoke from the burning oil and the left engine had stopped. They were going down in the middle of the fire. The hot air rising struck the Canadair shaking it up and down. Instead of resigning themselves and closing their eyes, as most people would have, Bruce remembered when he flew engineless planes, first paragliders and hang gliders, then ultralight aircraft. He began turning left over the fire, in very tight circles until he found a thermal, an updraft that lifted them. They reached two thousand meters altitude and with that they managed to glide to the lake where they made a water landing. That same day Commander Bruce went to see the boys in the hospital. Luckily none were seriously hurt and they all recovered in just a few days.

INVADERS
The invasion has begun
Jellyfish Invasion
Night of Day 16

Since I had a headlamp on, I didn't realize how late it was until I finally went out into the street. It was getting dark, it was almost nighttime and now the silence was momentarily broken by loud metallic sounds coming from one side or another in the distance. I took the precaution of turning off the flashlight and continued on my way back along the most sheltered side of the sidewalk. I heard noises everywhere and from what I had seen from the window of my house, I was starting to think maybe going out hadn't been a good idea; but what else could I have done, I was out of supplies. I passed by the charred bus lying across the middle of the street again. That's when I saw the blurred silhouettes in the gloom of two men crouched on the ground eating something. I froze when I realized they were two infected people literally eating the guts of a dead dog. My legs stuck to the ground, I was petrified and couldn't take another step. The handlebars slipped out of my sweaty hands and the bike hit the ground. This alerted the two beings who began to growl and look around, but they didn't seem to see me. They started sniffing like animals and came towards me. I immediately picked up the bike, took off and jumped on it, pedaling as fast as I could with the backpack on my back. The infected tried to follow me, but I quickly lost sight of them. I ran into the building entrance, grabbed the saddlebags from the mountain bike and went up loaded down by the stairs. There was no rest, now the terror again of going up the nine floors in the dark. Apparently, those creatures were more active at night. On the staircase landing, between the seventh and eighth floors, I heard noises again, this time I was sure they were footsteps. They may not have had good eyesight, but they had a good sense of smell. I couldn't turn on the flashlight or it would give away my position. So I put it in the chest pocket of my shirt and turned it on. The colored fabric filtered the light, dimming it but illuminating enough to see what was there. I saw three adult men, with tattered clothes, facing away, looking at the wall. I had to pass right by them without making any noise. I held my breath and tiptoed, but as I got near they got antsy, sniffing as if looking for a scent in the air. As soon as one of them turned around I took off running up the stairs as fast as I could while taking my house keys out of the pocket of my jeans. I was so nervous my hands were shaking and I couldn't manage to get the key in the lock. I closed my eyes and let my unconscious take over, I don't know how, but I managed to get it on the first try. I went in and closed the door just as those things were about to reach me.

INVADERS

The invasion has begun

Jellyfish Invasion

Day 17

Bruce was running down a main avenue, with a multitude of infected people on his heels. He was exhausted, he had been running for over an hour and couldn't shake them. They ran like demons, growling and drooling like rabid dogs. He saw the door to a building open and a man stuck half his body out yelling.

"Run, run, get in." - Eulalio helped Bruce get in and then closed the door.

"Thanks." - Bruce managed to say with great difficulty, still breathless.

"Good thing you're in shape, if they had caught you, they would have made short work of you." - Despite everything, Eulalio didn't seem to have lost his terrible sense of humor.

"Bruce." - And he shook his hand.

"Eulalio." - The other greeted back.

"What I'll never understand is why survivors trip each other up while the infected always help one another." - Eulalio looked at him in surprise. Until that moment he had never considered that.

Eulalio had an amateur radio station, with a long-range antenna deployed on the roof of the building. For several days there had been a repeating transmission. It was a series of numbers: 62.117493, -7.074099 He had written them down and checked them several times, but had no idea what it could be. He mentioned it to Bruce who, as soon as he saw the series of numbers, knew what it was.

"Latitude and longitude, they're coordinates, let's look on a map..."

Helped by a ruler, he marked the exact point with a pencil. It was the Faroe Islands. It was the only transmission he had picked up in all those days.

"We have to go there, if there are any survivors, an island may be the most suitable place to take refuge from the infected." - Eulalio looked at him as if he had lost his mind.

"And how are we going to get there? Swimming? It's best to stay here and wait for the army to come rescue us."

"No one is coming to rescue us, I was near a military base, they were the first to fall, infecting each other, strictly following the chain of command. There's an airport on the outskirts of the city, with a twin engine plane we can make it by the northern route, although we'll have to make some stops to refuel."

Given the idea of staying alone waiting for certain death, Eulalio took out backpacks and began filling them with necessities, water, cans of food, flashlight, batteries and a multi-purpose Swiss army knife.

"Okay, we'll leave in the morning, I've noticed those creatures are nocturnal, it's rare to see any of them during the day." - He still had doubts, he had seen those creatures literally eat his coworkers alive when he himself was reporting live from the news office.

"If we could get a working car..."

"I don't think a car would get us very far, the streets are full of obstacles: burnt out vehicles and all kinds of things. I have a Scrambler motorcycle that I rebuilt myself."

INVADERS
The invasion has begun
Jellyfish Invasion
Day 18

It was a very long night, I heard the blows the infected gave the door trying to get in. I reinforced it with furniture loaded with books, but the sounds, banging and growling made my hair stand on end. At dawn they left and I slept all morning, when I woke up I had some energy bars for breakfast, which made me feel much better. Then I took the soldering iron and solder and got to work. I dismantled one of the walkie-talkies, soldered the antenna wire to the receiver circuit and then the other end to the TV antenna junction box on the roof. By putting several batteries together I formed a twelve volt battery, three more than the radio said. I turned it on and searched for a signal changing one channel at a time. I did it several times until I finally picked up a faint transmission: 62.117493, -7.074099

The series of numbers was familiar to me, I picked up my cell phone which had a GPS app installed and when I entered the numbers it pointed to a small coastal village in the Faroe Islands. The GPS satellite triangulation was still working, it showed me the route from Madrid, crossing Spain, France, Belgium, Germany and Denmark, where I'd have to get on a boat. That route was beyond my reach, I knew how to pilot a boat, but not a large ship. I designed an alternative route, Madrid - France, cross from Calais to Dover, from there go up the UK, skirting London, Manchester, Glasgow and cross Scotland to Thurso, from there hopefully I could make it in a small boat to the Faroe Islands. Over the next two days I prepared everything and planned the trip in detail.

69

INVADERS
The invasion has begun
Jellyfish Invasion
Day 20

Knowing the habits of the infected, I left early in the morning. I crossed the city on the mountain bike, thanks to it I was able to bypass collapsed highways and roads full of wrecked vehicles. By 11:45 I was already in Alcalá de Henares and I realized that once outside the city, the roads were almost clear, some vehicles crashed in the ditches, but there was enough space to get through with a car. So I set about looking for suitable transportation, something I could be safe in at night. I thought of some kind of military all-terrain vehicle, when I was going down one of the streets on my bike I came across an armored van parked at the door of a bank branch. All the doors were open and the keys were in the ignition. I first checked that it had fuel and then turned the key all the way and it started right up. The keys also opened the rear doors giving access to the safe. There were bags of coins and bills everywhere, I made space by throwing everything into the street. As my mother used to say: If shit was worth money, the poor would be born without assholes. For once in my life I had bundles of five hundred euro bills in my hands and the money was worthless. I put the bike and backpack in the back and set off. It was a long trip, the van didn't go very fast, but I was very glad to have found it, I spent the nights inside the armored box and although infected people appeared from time to time and tried to get in by banging on it with their hands, they couldn't do anything. To sleep I put on headphones with music.

The French towns and cities were exactly the same, deserted as if a nuclear war had wiped out all human beings. I arrived in Calais at dusk, so I got out of the cab, went to the back, inserted the key in the rear door and froze when I felt a presence behind me. The first thing I thought was how stupid I had been, I shouldn't have gotten out of the van so late. This is as far as we go. It was only a matter of time, sooner or later I would make a mistake.

"Calm! Ne bouge pas!" - The voice in French was female.

I didn't understand French, but I almost jumped for joy at hearing someone speak after so long. When I turned around there was a police officer pointing a gun at my head. She was a young woman with very bright blue eyes.

"Fran, my name Fran."

"Oh, Spanish!" - She lowered the service weapon as soon as she realized I wasn't one of the infected.

INVADERS
The invasion has begun
Jellyfish Invasion
Day 21

Lucrèce spoke some Spanish, so mixing it with English and some words in French, we managed to understand each other. She was the last of her police unit, the first days of the epidemic they were sent with the military to try to contain the infected. But the virus spread so quickly that soon everyone got sick. She had been walking for many days, taking refuge at night in abandoned houses. The first thing she did was go to her parents' house, to check if they were okay, but there was no one there. I told her my plan and she helped me cross over to Dover, she knew how to start up a boat and navigate well. We arrived on the English coast early in the morning and spent the whole day looking for a safe vehicle. The best we found was a refrigerated truck. At dusk, we locked ourselves in from the inside with padlocks. That night there wasn't a sound. We had candles, plenty of food, a bottle of very expensive French wine, accompanied by a tray of cheeses. We talked all night, at first about what had happened, the infected and how to get to the Faroe Islands; then the conversation became trivial and informal, we even got around to telling jokes. When I realized we were kissing. She seemed like the most beautiful woman in the world to me - And maybe she was -.

It dawned drizzling, the sky was gray and cloudy. With the truck we moved towards the outskirts of London, there we changed transportation, we got an armored military vehicle, an armored vehicle with large all-terrain wheels. With the armored vehicle we could even drive at night, because any infected person who had the bad idea of getting in our way was crushed like a cockroach. We realized there were fewer and fewer of them and if they appeared it was in much smaller groups. Maybe they were killing each other, the disease was killing them or they were simply starving to death.

Eric the aerospace engineer
Rockets

Five, four, three, two, one, ignition, Eric pressed the red button and the rocket shot out like a lightning bolt, reaching great height. A digital display on the ground showed how high it climbed. It was a perfect launch, it flew splendidly, with no vibrations or deviations from its trajectory, reaching the expected distance. A complete success that Eric would celebrate with his colleague Martín. Eric was an aeronautical engineer and a rocket enthusiast, he was possibly one of the best at designing and manufacturing them. But it was a profession without profit, so to support his family he worked in a factory designing plastic household products. He dedicated his free time to building small rockets. With them he tested new ideas: improvements in fuel pumps, advances in guidance systems and more efficient thrusters. In short, he applied all kinds of ideas that could improve the design to reach greater height more cheaply and reliably.

Eric lived in the Faroe Islands, he was a middle-aged man with reddish hair and very white skin. He had a good beer belly, like any good beer drinker. He always wore long-sleeved shirts and wool sweaters.

INVADERS

The invasion has begun
Jellyfish Invasion
Day 29

The fog dissipated as we entered the horseshoe-shaped bay of the small town of Kvivik Church, revealing the green, grassy mountains surrounding a group of small houses, with walls and roofs of red, black and green colors. The white bell tower with gray tiles of the small church stood out in the center. Lucrèce stopped the boat as close as possible to the houses. I helped tie it up and we walked through the streets of the town, not knowing where to go. Again the absolute stillness that kept me on alert. We moved towards the center until we reached the church doors. Through the windows I thought I saw movement inside. Lucrèce drew her Glock 17 pistol, positioned herself on the side of the main door and signaled me to be quiet and stand behind her. She pushed open the door and entered the church with the gun out front. Inside there were almost a hundred people, the community was gathered around a woman. Everyone fell silent.

"Please, lower the gun and come closer." - Said Dr. Maria Garcia signaling to some empty seats for them to sit down.

She explained in English everything they had learned in the Hesperides lab. At her side was Commander Bruce and Eulalio the journalist.

INVADERS
The invasion has begun
Jellyfish Invasion
The Island

The Faroe Islands are the islands of sheep, located in the North Atlantic between Scotland and Iceland and are an autonomous country that belongs to the Kingdom of Denmark. Being far from the continent in such northern waters and separated into seventeen small islands, its population of almost fifty thousand inhabitants was not initially affected by the pandemic, until an infected sailor arrived in Tórshavn, the capital, spreading the virus. The entire population, more than twelve thousand people, became infected. The rest of the towns and cities on the different islands remained safe. Its mountainous, green terrain lacks forests and almost all resources arrive through fishing. Since the jellyfish plague, boats had remained moored in port. In the cities of Klaksvík, with a population of about four thousand five hundred people, Hoyvík with more than three thousand, Argir with almost two thousand and Fuglafjorður with one thousand five hundred citizens, there began to be a shortage of food and medicine. The rest of the locations called bygd, rural communities, villages and towns were self-sufficient. One way or another, once the project was approved and construction of the aircraft began, huge amounts of materials were needed. A group of men would have to travel to the continent to get them. That would not have been possible if not for Fran's discovery and Dr. Garcia's experiments. Now the men in charge of bringing the necessary materials and supplies, in addition to being clad in police, military and sports armor, also carried a special cocktail of medications prepared by the doctor to prevent infection in case they were bitten.

It is said that the first settlers arrived fleeing tyrannical kings, there is talk of monks from Scotland who settled there, Norwegians escaping King Harald I also found refuge there. However, there is evidence that Norse settlers had arrived much earlier, as they were the ones who brought the language that gave rise to the current language spoken on the islands. Once again the Faroes served as a refuge for those fleeing the continent. Because they are not members of the European Union, the containment measures carried out by the army did not include the islands. It was the armed forces, the military personnel who moved from one side to the other, who in a way helped spread the virus. On the other hand, NATO has a radar station in Mjorkadalur, belonging to the Arctic polar radar network. Along with the thirteen FM radio stations and one AM station at 531 kHz, it made it an exceptional enclave to carry out the project. Despite its very northern geographical location, its climate is oceanic, due to the predominant temperate Gulf Stream. With a mild climate considering its latitude. The thermometer fluctuates all year between the minimum winter temperature of half a degree Celsius and eleven in summer. On the contrary, fog and wind are common companions.

INVADERS
The invasion has begun
Jellyfish Invasion
Day 30

They gathered around a table in the local pub, Maria, Bruce, Eulalio, Lucrèce and Francisco, wanted to know how things were going outside, Lucrèce and Fran knew firsthand about the situation in Europe, in Spain, France and England. But the doctor's curiosity went further, she wanted to know if at some point they had had contact with the infected and if so, why they had not developed the disease. In this regard, Fran had a lot to contribute. He recounted that before the outbreak he had gone scuba diving and had been stung by many jellyfish, at night he had a high fever and instead of taking modern analgesics, he took a large dose of acetylsalicylic acid. This interested the doctor.

That same night, Dr. Maria Garcia performed some tests, using the small island doctor's clinic as a lab. She sprayed a tiny jellyfish with the acid and shortly after it changed from a reddish color to a normal white color. Then she put it in contact with a mouse and found that nothing else happened, it no longer had or transmitted the disease. It was the first time she had something to work with. Recently infected people treated properly could survive. The next morning at a new meeting in the church she reported this and distributed acetylsalicylic acid to everyone. She gave instructions to take it immediately in case of contact with jellyfish, animals or infected people. It was the first time they had something to fight the pandemic. Unfortunately for more than ninety percent of the world's population it was too late.

"It's the only way we have to face the virus. As long as the sea remains full of those jellyfish, there's nothing we can do."

Bruce raised his hand as if he were in school, Maria gave him the floor.

"You said the jellyfish was no longer toxic when it received the acid dose."

"That's right."

"What if we sprayed them from an airplane?"

"Where? They're everywhere."

"You said the Artika and Hesperides detected the breeding area... Maybe if we released a large amount of that product over the area, we'd accomplish something." - The doctor thought motionless for a moment.

"Nonsense!" - The mayor interjected.

"No, it's not nonsense, it could work."

They immediately began making calculations with the data the doctor had. Eric the engineer joined the group. They calculated the amount of acid that would have to be transported and released in the north. The figure discussed was one thousand tons. The world's largest cargo plane, the Antonov An-225, could only carry 180 tons and for the plan to be effective all the acid had to be released at the exact point at the same time. Then Eric, the aerospace engineer, had an idea.

Commander Bruce's Flight Logs

They say the ancients dedicated the seventh day to giving thanks to the sun and that spring Sunday it shone brightly. The air show was held the first weekend of every month. With good weather the stands were packed with people. Cereal fields extended in all directions as far as the eye could see; green fields, red with poppies and white with daisies. As if planted for that very purpose, each plot of land was predominantly one species. The central runway of the airfield was narrow and paved, the grass sides were used by lighter aircraft. While the children ran and played around the stands, parents lined up near the hangars, where there was a stand selling hot dogs, freshly baked rolls, with strips of pickles and crunchy onion dressed with a special house mustard sauce. Nothing like those fluorescent yellow premade sauces. Dark in color it had an intense yet smooth flavor. Surely most of the children came to see the airplanes and most parents came for the food and drink. Accompanying the hot dogs with craft beer or natural fruit slushies.

First the oldest planes came out, which were gradually followed by more modern, advanced models, up to present day ones. Those old piston engine airplanes captivated the hearts of older attendees and the imaginations of younger ones. Each had its own peculiar charm, the sound of its engines, its shapes and its flight. I suppose the kind of mystical magic felt by the first people who saw them fly is still latent in their engines today, equally captivating people who watch them.

She looked at the planes as if they were living beings, pampered them and sometimes even spoke to them. Once she told Bruce: People are born with a soul, a set defined by their feelings and emotions;

some objects carefully manufactured by men accumulate the feelings and emotions of the people who loved them and end up having their own soul. Susan always went out to the runway smiling, she got on her old Bücker Bü 131 Jungmann and looked as happy as a child. She performed one of the most complicated aerial acrobatics maneuvers. The propeller era was over, it was already part of the past, of other times when flying was an art and not a science. Now the noisy jet fighters reigned in the sky, leaving the wonderful piston engine airplanes forgotten. After decades of ruling the skies, now their glory days were relegated to the few days when they were brought out to fly for nostalgic dreamers' delight. It was almost Bruce's turn and he carefully checked all the components and structure of his airplane, a flaming red biplane. With it he could perform any figure he imagined in the air. Delighting children and adults alike. His number ended with tight crosses in which he and Susan's planes almost touched. They had met in a complicated situation: That day he was in charge of the airfield, the facilities were closed for repairs, there were pits and construction fences all over the runway. Out of nowhere a biplane made a very low pass, intending to land, Bruce waved his arms for it to climb again and leave. But the pilot ignored him, and landed his Bücker on the taxiway between the hangars and the runway. When she got out of the plane, Bruce yelled at her calling her crazy.

"Didn't you see me signaling? Are you crazy?"

Susan took off her leather helmet and aviation goggles and was speechless when she saw such a pretty woman.

"I'm sorry, my tank is dry, I don't have a drop of fuel left." - Light green eyes and a beautiful smile on her mouth.

For the first time he was speechless, it was love at first sight and when he finally managed to articulate something he only said nonsense, which fortunately made Susan laugh. She was petite, with very light green eyes and curly blonde hair. But when she got on her airplane she became a fantastic aviator. He helped her refuel, when they finished loading the fuel it was already night and she would have to wait until morning to take off.

"If you want I can drive you to town in my car, there you can stay overnight at an inn."

"Thanks, but I'm not leaving my old friend alone, if you don't mind we'll spend the night here."

"Over there in front of that wooden cabin, we have the office, there's an armchair, wood stove, drink and food."

They spent the night talking about planes and were surprised by the morning sun, naked in each other's arms on the couch.

They would go on after the oldest planes, in a kind of intermission between the old and the new, the classic and the modern. They had performed that routine hundreds of times, it was controlled risk. After the inspection he climbed into the cockpit and made strange hand movements, it was the way aerobatic pilots memorized each of the figures they would perform in the air. Their departure was announced over the PA system, he put on the headset and connected it to the radio. He gave the throttle a few pumps, released the brakes and taxied down the taxiway until lining up at the threshold. Before taking off, he took a stick of gum out of his jacket pocket and folded it as he put it in his mouth. At takeoff all the built up tension disappeared, staying on the ground. They put on a formidable performance and accelerated the planes towards each other, as if they were going to crash into each other. They made several close crosses, so close he could see the green brightness of Susan's eyes. It all happened very quickly, in just one instant, he felt something in his chest, as if something was wrong and when exiting one of the maneuvers, the engine on his biplane lost power. When it slowed down Susan couldn't avoid him and their wings touched. The structure burst and both planes fell to the ground in flames. Bruce with a broken leg managed to get out of his, but when he limped towards Susan's it exploded. That was the last time he saw her. She disappeared with her plane, completely devoured by the fire. Although the investigating committee determined it had been a mechanical failure, Bruce always blamed himself for what happened.

84

INVADERS
The invasion has begun
Jellyfish Invasion
Beginning of the Project

The project was about to fail, even before it began. The island authorities opposed the construction of the airship, thinking it was a useless waste of resources. Bruce stood up and began telling a story:

Many were the brave ones who tried to break the sound barrier, to exceed number one on the scoreboard, most died trying. Upon reaching point nine on the mach meter, the plane's controls would start shaking violently, the whole aircraft would start shaking. The screws came loose, the clock hands went crazy and the plane went into a tailspin. The controls didn't respond and they finally ended up crashing into the ground. Pilots lost consciousness due to the violent spins they underwent. The few who managed to stay conscious saw the wings burst from the pressure. Jumping by parachute was impossible, even in the unlikely event that the aviator managed to open the cockpit - the air at that speed is like a concrete wall. - there was no way to detach oneself from the seat. Scientists said the speed of sound was a physical barrier, a barrier no man would manage to exceed. The pilots said that at mach one you experience the demon of the wind and it devours anyone who ventures into its domains. The few pilots who managed to graze one on the speed dial and returned said they had seen the demon stalking them, trying to hunt them down. A man-eating monster that would not allow anyone to enter its kingdom. The stories about that demon spread like wildfire, but test pilots were another kind of man. People for whom risking their lives and putting themselves on the line was part of their daily job. They didn't believe in that demon, or any other and fully trusted their skills to defy the laws of physics.

"So don't tell me what can or can't be done." - Commander Bruce blurted it out to the faces of all those who did not believe it was possible to build an aircraft capable of transporting the cargo north and dropping it in the jellyfish breeding center.

The project to destroy the virus

Building an aircraft was an arduous and complicated task, even for an experienced team. I had participated in the construction of several airplanes, first one made of wood, similar to model airplanes but on a larger scale. The next we made of fiberglass and carbon fiber, it was complicated to learn to use composite materials, chemicals and resins. We also built several autogyros, the reconstruction of a Robinson R22 helicopter. All of that had given me quite a bit of experience and I knew how complicated a project of that nature was. Fortunately this time the team had several experts.

Different methods were considered for carrying the acid load to the jellyfish breeding site. Antonov AN-225 cargo planes might have been a good option, in the hypothetical case of having a fleet of them and an army of pilots who knew how to fly them. Arriving by boat had been impossible even for the Hesperides and Artika, a super icebreaker with its entire crew was needed. Exposing them again to contagion from being in contact with the water. Finally the small commission of experts agreed to build an airship, which could carry the entire load at once and drop it on ground zero. We only needed that contraption to work once, a single one-way flight for the crew, pilot and copilot. In this case Bruce and me.

Preparing for the mission

I barely slept at all throughout the night, I couldn't stop thinking about how the flight would go. I repeated to myself over and over the things I had to do, trying to memorize it. Yesterday had been hard, a lot of work and little rest, I needed to sleep to feel good the next morning. With the nerves I couldn't fall asleep.

Construction of the aircraft

With the team prepared, construction of the zeppelin began. On the drawing table we discarded many prototypes until finally settling on one that seemed suitable to carry out the mission. In a field behind the hangars we set up a metal structure that we later covered with canvas. It was like a modular tent, but on an infinitely larger scale. We started building the zeppelin. There were many naysayers, detractors who thought the effort wasn't worth it, the expenditure of resources, as if staying hidden at home would cause the epidemic to subside and the world to return to normal. Doing nothing was just waiting for certain death. Despite the setbacks, construction continued.

INVADERS
The invasion has begun
Jellyfish Invasion
Back on the continent

The vast majority of Faroe Islanders were seasoned sailors. Many were dedicated to cod fishing. They had a good fleet, captains and sailors. They used one of the ferries that make the crossing from Denmark to the islands. A group of volunteers departed for the continent. They were divided into several teams, each with a particular mission. Accompanying them in command were Dr. Garcia, Bruce, Lucrèce and Fran, as they were the people with the most experience on how to move forward in a post-apocalyptic world facing the infected. When they arrived at the port of Hirtshals early in the morning, prepared to disembark, they realized the desolation, the lack of movement and noise. Time seemed to have stopped, but a more detailed look revealed the catastrophe, wrecked vehicles, next to burnt buildings. They had to move quickly before it got late and the infected appeared. The different teams, clad in proper attire, police and military armor, helmets and tall boots, commandeered various vehicles. Fran and Lucrèce headed to a nearby warehouse in search of the helium bottles needed for the zeppelin's buoyancy.

The two groups had special forces police, armed and prepared to repel any attack. Special forces with heavier weapons also remained on the ship.

Team Bravo

The convoy made up of three large tractor-trailer trucks and an armored police van crossed the city until reaching the warehouse marked on the map. They found nothing but desolation everywhere. The warehouses seemed intact, with the rolled down metal shutters closing the doors. Lucrèce ordered one of the truck drivers to turn around and back up, to knock down the shutter with the rear of the trailer. The assault team went in first, when they checked the area was secure, they signaled for the men to get out of the vehicles and get to work. The warehouse was full of bottles, there were many more than they needed. The forklifts worked perfectly and greatly facilitated loading the trucks. The large gas bottle storage warehouse was damp, cold and dark. Lucrèce had a bad feeling, the place was suitable for the infected, as if built to their very taste.

"We have to leave now!" - She spoke half in English and French. Fran understood her perfectly. "It's getting dark."

"Thirty bottles are missing, without them the zeppelin won't be able to fly..."

They loaded the remaining helium, unfortunately dropping the last shipment when putting it on the truck bed. A cylinder fell from up high, fortunately it didn't explode, although helium is not a flammable gas, the high pressure in the cylinders is enough to explode and injure the men standing around. The noise of metal on metal sounded louder than a cathedral bell. Before leaving the warehouse infected people suddenly appeared arriving in droves from the city, attracted by the noise. The police snipers began making accurate shots hitting the infected in the head. There were so many that they managed to knock down and break through the rear fence, entering through the narrow alleys until reaching the main door, taking four of the police by surprise. Among them was the radio operator, in charge of communicating with the ship. There were about twenty and they ended up knocking the police to the floor. The snipers couldn't do anything, if they fired they could hit their own men.

Team Alpha

Bruce was trying to communicate by radio with Team Bravo, he got no response. It was getting dark and infected were appearing everywhere.

"No response from Fran and Lucrèce's group." - He told Maria and kept trying.

They had to raise the loading platform gate. Snipers prepared to open fire with precision rifles equipped with telescopic sights and also larger caliber repeating weapons. Maria ordered not to fire unless absolutely necessary, she knew that once the shooting started, the noise would attract all the infected within a radius of several kilometers. The hundreds of infected began crowding against the ferry's gate. They began climbing like ants, insects, over each other. When the first of them poked his head over the edge, a bullet went through his eye killing him instantly, if you could consider those things to have life. With the rifle's bang, the growls increased and new monsters appeared everywhere. Soon the machine guns had to open fire.

"We have to leave now, or we'll all die." - Said the ferry captain.

"We'll hold out as long as we can." - Bruce answered gruffly. "You're not a child, we're all risking our skins here."

Shell casings rolled around the deck piling up. At that rate they would run out of ammo in a few minutes.

"Nothing, they don't answer." - Bruce said again after another attempt with the radio.

"I'm not leaving here without the helium." - Replied the doctor.

Team Bravo

Lucrèce pulled out her Glock and unloaded her eleven bullets at point blank range into the heads of the infected. She threw the magazine on the floor and put in a new one she took out of her tactical vest pocket. She made another eleven precise shots and the four men got up off the floor, removing the pile of corpses from on top of them. The radio was destroyed, they couldn't communicate with the ship, but that was the least of their worries now. They got into the vehicles and all the men who had been in contact with the infected took a large dose of the medications prepared by Dr. Maria.

Team Alpha-Bravo

They were about to give up when they saw the convoy's lights entering the port. The trucks honked and the infected moved away from the boat towards them.

"Open the hatches." - Bruce shouted.

The trucks entered the ship's cargo bay, plowing through the infected. After closing the hatches, the elite commandos eliminated all those who had managed to get inside.

INVADERS

The invasion has begun

Jellyfish Invasion

The Mission

1

Bruce was at the controls, the co-pilot or second in command was Lucrèce, Dr. Maria and Francisco also accompanied them, in charge of the proper functioning of all systems, electronic, electrical, hydraulic and mechanical, including the condition of the engines. Once they were in the zero zone, he would be in charge of opening the tank valves and releasing the acid.

The day dawned gray, early autumn the weather was beginning to change, they had to leave as soon as possible or they wouldn't have another chance until next summer. It was impossible to fly so far north in winter, even less so with an aircraft of that nature. The great zeppelin was greatly affected by the wind, it could blow it off course laterally or leave it motionless, pinned in one spot unable to advance if blowing against it. To avoid this problem, they had built the gigantic dirigible with an aerodynamic shape, it resembled a huge manta ray and unlike models from the early twentieth century, it barely had an interior structure. The new composite materials, carbon fiber and resins, facilitated construction and allowed the design to be flipped. The exterior was rigid and the concept similar to that of an egg, the thin shell withstands all the pressure. The paint glimmered in the sun like the pearly interior of a mussel shell, due to its photovoltaic properties, the entire surface of the device functioned as a huge solar panel, producing electricity for the engines. The zeppelin's cruising speed was one hundred twenty kilometers per hour, reaching the drop point would take several days. The mission, if everything went according to plan, would last a week. Dr. Maria Garcia would be responsible for identifying the right place to drop the acid. She was the only person who had been in the jellyfish breeding area. The aircraft's cabin was prepared to accommodate four people, they had a bunk bed built into the back, which they would take turns using to rest. Food and drink for seven days, if the mission was prolonged they would have to ration it. The thousands of island inhabitants had contributed to a greater or lesser extent to the development of the project. Hundreds of people approached to see the contraption take off. Bruce and Lucrèce activated the switches to release ballast and the formidable wing took off slowly and steadily. They took off with some fog that had formed around the island, then the sky cleared, the sun shone all day, it was such nice weather it seemed they were on an excursion. But at night with the drop in temperatures they had the first problems. Lucrèce who was controlling the ship while Bruce rested, felt a strong jolt and they began falling uncontrollably. Bruce performed some tests on the controls, something was destabilizing the zeppelin. He realized the temperature had dropped drastically. He turned on the powerful forward landing lights and saw small white flashes all over the sky, it was very fine snow. He reversed the engines on the right side, applying full power against the left one. That way they came out of the tailspin, but they kept descending.

"Snow and ice must have accumulated on the fuselage, then strong wind must have detached the layer on one side, leaving all the weight on the other. I don't know how long I can keep it like this, you'll have to get out through the top hatches and remove the ice with shovels."

Bruce stayed at the controls while Lucrèce, Maria and Fran went outside. In case repairs were needed, they had tools, safety harnesses and climbing ropes. Outside there was terrible wind and the cold froze you instantly. You had to clip on with carabiners to the work area so as not to fall into the void. The task was complicated by the situation and the large area they had to clean. They worked on the farthest area to stabilize the wing as soon as possible. Bruce had become overconfident due to the good weather and instead of flying at a higher altitude, above the clouds, they remained too low, unaware that the weather had changed. The aircraft the size of several football fields had not been designed to fly with that additional load on the fuselage. The engines at full power were consuming all the battery charge. If they managed to get rid of the ice and not crash into the middle of the Arctic Ocean, they would spend the rest of the night adrift until the sun recharged the batteries again. They managed to remove a good part of the accumulated snow and ice. Then the doctor unclipped her carabiner to carefully move to another place to continue working. Fran was closer to the center of the wing and when he thrust his shovel into the half meter thick layer, he heard a crack, as if the carbon fiber shell had cracked. But he soon realized it wasn't that, a plaque several tens of meters across had come loose; the air did the rest, the plaque moved violently sweeping the doctor with it. Lucrèce who was closer, unclipped her carabiner and ran to try to save her. She dove and slid across the smooth surface, just managing to touch her with her fingertips, but couldn't grab her. Maria was heard screaming as she was lost into the darkness of the night falling into the void. They gave her up for dead, but soon heard her screams. She had gotten caught hanging from the main rope. With great effort and care they managed to hoist her up. They were careful not to let the rope get cut on any sharp edges. The zeppelin regained altitude. Once back inside the cabin, Bruce gave them the bad news, the batteries were dead and the night would be very long, drifting at the mercy of the wind and periodically going out to check for more ice buildup.

99

INVADERS
The invasion has begun
Jellyfish Invasion
The Mission

2

The wind had diverted it quite a bit from the route, but they were thankful just to still be alive. The zeppelin's photovoltaic shell was very efficient and in a few hours with the little light filtering through the clouds, it minimally charged the batteries, enough to rise above the storm. At ten thousand meters altitude, the sky looked completely clear and below the clouds formed a dense, fluffy white mantle like cotton.

"How's everything going?" - Fran asked Bruce and Lucrèce as she handed each a cup of coffee.

She told Lucrèce to rest for a bit, that she would relieve her. Bruce had the habit of dozing a bit reclining the pilot's seat. At that altitude, he could rest while Fran took care of not deviating from the route.

"We've deviated a lot from the route, losing almost twenty hours. But luckily we're all okay." - He made a worried gesture pointing with his eyes at Dr. Maria who was resting in the bunk in the back.

The rest of the day went by without incident, they ate, drank and rested, and even had time to chat, an inconsequential conversation, favorite music and movies, they didn't comment on the mission at all.

"Do you think the world will go back to how it was before?" - The doctor thought about Fran's words. "What reason could there be for what has happened?"

"Nature always finds a way to survive, to defend itself from external aggressions. Humans have been destroying it for centuries and this has been its response. The way to shake us off. " - That's how she saw it. "If we get another chance, I hope we don't make the same mistakes again."

INVADERS
The invasion has begun
Jellyfish Invasion
The Mission

3

On the third day they flew at a good pace, crossing the slight inert air above the clouds. The aircraft was designed precisely for that, to fly higher than any airplane could. Eric, the engineer, devised this kind of modern zeppelin to transport a large load as high as possible. A floating platform from which to launch a rocket into space more cheaply and efficiently. Below them the gigantic storm was becoming more virulent, the nearly black gray clouds were approaching them. The continuous electrical discharges seemed like bombardment. The extreme weather conditions produced an unusual phenomenon, the lightning flashes shot rays into the stratosphere.

"Lucrèce, divert all power to the main engines, we need to get out of here as soon as possible." - The commander gave instructions and when he got so serious, it was obvious the situation must be more dangerous than it initially appeared.

Bruce made several maneuvers, complicated turns, but there was no way to escape the storm. Lightning struck the hull. All electronic systems shut off. So now they were flying visually. The pilot took a map from his pocket, placed it on his right thigh and with a pencil began making notes, all while piloting through the electrical storm trying to dodge the ascending lightning bolts.

"Maria, take my place." - Lucrèce got up from the co-pilot's seat giving it to her.

Fran and she went down a narrow hallway to a kind of small living room where the batteries were located and where all the aircraft's electrical wires and circuits converged. Before arriving, the hallway was already filled with black smoke. They grabbed fire extinguishers and fought the flames coming out of the batteries and electrical hoses. They took several more hits and while fighting the fire the zeppelin shook violently, rolling them on the floor. They were in a steep prolonged nosedive. It was hard to breathe, their battered, sore bodies from the bruising and their blurry vision. They put out the fire and stumbled back to the cabin.

"Why are we descending?" - Fran asked, holding her hand to her forehead due to the headache and dizziness.

"Lightning opened a breach in the hull depressurizing the ship. If we don't descend quickly, we'll run out of oxygen and die of asphyxiation."

"Can we still complete the mission?"

"Right now the important thing is getting out of this, surviving at least for the moment and then we'll see what we do."

They were suffocating, it was getting harder and harder for them to breathe. The dizziness and nausea increased to the point that Fran lost consciousness. Then the two women also fainted, Bruce was trained and seasoned as an acrobatic pilot and managed to stay at the controls. As they descended, breathable air entered and they recovered after a few minutes. The zeppelin now sailed through the storm, shaken and with continuous course changes. Then almost the same way it all started, calm suddenly arrived. Now the fog seemed less dense. Bruce had recorded every course change on the map.

"Did we make it?" - The doctor relieved on one hand and worried on the other.

"The ship is solid and holds up, but now we can't fly high due to cabin decompression. The fog prevents the photovoltaic cells from charging the batteries, so soon we'll run out of thrusters and fly lost adrift."

"Where are we?" - Maria asked.

Bruce circled an area on the map with his pencil, indicating where they were located. The doctor took a good look.

"We're flying over the area where the Hesperides was left. If we could descend further, we'd be able to see them."

"I don't understand you."

"The only way to continue the mission is to fly above the fog to have power to the engines. We're not far from the ground zero area now."

"I already said we can't go up, the lack of oxygen would kill us."

"That's the key, if we could descend on the Hesperides, we could get oxygen tanks and masks from the lab."

INVADERS
The invasion has begun
Jellyfish Invasion
The Mission

4

The commander descended and ordered everyone to look out the windows, searching for the ship. Visibility was very poor, they circled around, but couldn't find it. They didn't have energy for much longer.

"There, there's something there." - Everyone looked where Fran was pointing.

As they got closer, the vision cleared and a ghost ship appeared out of the fog, trapped in the Arctic ice.

"It's the Artika." - The doctor confirmed. "The Hesperides has to be very close, a little more to the west."

Shortly after, the other ship appeared, covered in a white ice layer. Bruce executed the approach maneuver. The aircraft was not designed to land. The pilot's skill managed to get the zeppelin hovering twenty meters above the Hesperides. The ship trapped in the ice and frozen appeared to have been there for a hundred years. From the cargo hold, Francisco, Lucrèce and the doctor descended in a metal basket connected to a lift used for loading and unloading. The cable descended vertically onto the ship, leaving the three on deck. The ground was frozen and slippery. This time they were not prepared to face infected people, there were no plans to make any stops or excursions to the Hesperides. They wore special warm clothing, but nothing more, no defenses or weapons, not even Lucrèce's Glock; Bruce emphasized this, having a weapon inside a pressurized vessel was not a good idea. Who would think they would have to descend onto a ship full of infected people. From what they had seen, it was possible there were none left, that the virus carriers had died of starvation or been devoured by the disease itself. The doctor was the only one who knew the way, so she led the group. They walked in silence, tried to open one of the hatches but it was impossible because the locking mechanism was completely frozen. They had to change plans and enter from the opposite side, having to take a longer route inside the ship. The only flashlight was carried by the doctor, taking care to tape the bulb to dim the light and avoid attracting the infected people's attention. They crossed through the lounge, Maria paused looking at the table with the green cloth that had a poker deck and poker chips; she remembered the game they played before everyone got infected by the virus. It seemed like a thousand years ago, a distant dream, her own life, her memories seemed to belong to someone else. The world was no longer the same, or what was left of it. The interior of the Hesperides was dark and icy, the generators must have stopped long ago, everything was covered in frost. Breathing froze their lungs and exhaled breath turned into frozen vapor. It smelled musty, damp and rotten. The silence was absolute, the only thing heard was their footsteps, the creaking of the frozen carpet under their feet. They reached the hallway intersection and she remembered her friend Dr. Lee Oneal, she felt sorrow for leaving her on the deck of the Artika. The memory engraved in her mind of her boat moving away and the woman raising her hand in a final farewell. The hallway intersection was clear and they soon arrived at the lab doors. They communicated with hand signals to avoid making noise. They went inside and loaded up with as many oxygen tanks as they could carry, one in each hand, the doctor carried the largest one, which had a pull handle and little wheels. They were about to head back when they saw something moving quickly in the dark. When Maria Garcia shined her flashlight on the area, Tim lunged at her. Timothy Hannan, or rather what was left of him, as pieces of flesh were missing all over his face, he was completely deformed and unrecognizable. There was no time to act, before they could do anything, Tim or what was left of him had pounced on the doctor and when she put her arms up to try to push him away he took several bites. Blood dripped down her arms. Maria's screams of pain were heard throughout the ship. Lucrèce was right next to her and grabbing the oxygen tank tightly used it to hit the infected man on the head. Blow after blow as if it were a mace, she crushed Timothy's head or what was left of it until smashing it turning it into a kind of mush or puree.

"We have to get out of here as soon as possible." - Said Maria wrapping her bitten arms with adhesive tape.

Noises and growls were coming from all over the Hesperides. They ran down the hallways towards the exit but found their way blocked by a large number of infected people running at them. They had to take the corridor in the other direction, to the exit of the door that was blocked. Now the main thing was to escape the rabid infected people, then they would think about how to get out onto the deck. When they reached another hallway intersection, Dr. Maria Garcia stopped for a moment falling behind, she set the alarm on her pink silicone sports watch, threw it as far as possible down the left hallway and kept running to catch up with Fran and Lucrèce. The Casio started beeping, a shrill, annoying sound and all the infected people went towards it. Once at the frozen door, they tried unsuccessfully to open it again. They tried pushing the steering wheel that unlocks the lock, but it was useless. Then Fran took off his jacket and put the cotton sweater against the lock, then lit it on fire with a lighter. The timid flame barely produced some heat, then he brought the mouth of one of the oxygen bottles close and opened it onto the fire. Huge flames formed and the metal door turned orange from the heat. Then covering his hands with the jacket, he easily opened the door and they ran across the frozen deck hearing the growls of the infected people who arrived attracted by the strong smell of burning. Bruce who saw them through the cabin window lowered the aircraft onto the ship, the metal basket of the lift hit the deck forcefully. The infected ran like possessed people towards them. The three got into the basket and the commander quickly gained altitude. Two infected managed to grab onto the basket and with their weight prevented the lift motor from pulling them up. The cable could snap at any moment and the basket tip over due to the strong swaying. As best they could, with kicks and punches, Lucrèce and Francisco managed to knock them off.

INVADERS

The invasion has begun

Jellyfish Invasion

The Mission

5

After what had happened Fran always carried a box of Aspirin with him. He gave the doctor the box and she took two together. She was starting to feel sick, had a fever and nausea. They helped her into bed and covered her with a blanket. Everyone wore a transparent mask connected to the oxygen bottle. Having to wear the mask and oxygen bottle all the time was very annoying. They gained altitude again above the clouds and got enough energy for the thrusters. The photovoltaic cells covering the entire hull had been badly damaged by the lightning strikes. Navigation without electronic instruments was very complicated, especially at night. They were almost over ground zero and the doctor was getting worse by the moment, tremors and cold sweats, accompanied by delirious words and phrases that made no sense. Fran was in charge of continuing to give her the medications diluted in orange juice. The sun disk appeared in a black sky that from the height they were at made them feel like they were in space. Against all odds, they had managed to reach the drop zone. The ship was very damaged, they might not make it back. They had to descend to release the acid, then they wouldn't have enough energy to climb, nor did they have enough oxygen for the return trip. Despite all the preparations the mission had become a one way trip. The most likely outcome was that they would die on the way back, like Captain Robert Falcon Scott and his men.

"What do we do with her?" - The three spoke softly about the doctor's condition. "She's getting worse by the minute."

"Are you giving her the medications?" - The situation was getting out of hand.

Lucrèce said it would be best to tie her to the bed for whatever might happen, for their safety, hers, and the mission's. They agreed. They tied her with pieces of cloth cut from a sheet so she wouldn't hurt herself. Fran was in charge of continuing to give her the crushed pills diluted in juice. The oxygen bottles were about to run out.

"Okay, the moment of truth has arrived." - Bruce lowered the zeppelin. "Get to your stations, we only have one chance and can't fail."

They entered the dense fog again, the pilot slowly descended the last stretch until able to see ground zero. In the ice floe a perfectly circular crater had opened in the ice. Something seemed to generate a heat source there. It could have been some kind of underwater volcanic eruption, creating hot liquid fumaroles. The other more puzzling option was that powerful multinationals were competing for Arctic mineral resources. Bruce had heard about a prototype thermal drill powered by a small nuclear reactor. When they descended further, they could see the workers' facilities and machinery. The secret, illegal drilling, hidden from public view, had drilled onto the surface of a frozen lake. A huge underground lake isolated for thousands of years. In Antarctica similar experiments were being conducted in subglacial Lake Vostok. But here they had jumped all laws and legislation, using the huge atomic drill, disregarding the consequences. The three were surprised to see the extensive facilities and the huge platform holding the drill arm in the center of the lake. It seems the isolated waters of the subglacial lake contained some kind of unknown life, perhaps its own microbial fauna. The rest was easy to imagine, contamination upon opening Pandora's box was assured, the heat produced by the drill created small vessels, underground rivers under the ice, small capillaries that connected the lake to the Arctic Ocean.

With great skill Bruce placed the damaged aircraft over the lake and gave the order to release the acid. If Dr. Maria Garcia's theory was correct, in the same way that the jellyfish had become infected and spread the virus throughout the planet, now they would do the reverse, transmitting the antidote. They dropped the load.

"Congratulations we have accomplished the mission!" - The three hugged.

There was no celebration, a race against the clock began to try to get back home. Without oxygen, they couldn't climb to fly above the fog and without instrumentation or visibility, finding the way back was impossible. The engines were running on minimum. They could crash at any moment, he didn't know the altitude they were flying at. The only chance was to find a way to get through the fog and out of it. Without realizing it they were circling around. At some point the engines would completely fail and they would fall into the frozen ocean. The heating in the cockpit was the first thing that stopped working due to lack of power. Inside everything was frozen, they withstood thanks to the special jackets they wore. But it was so cold that little by little they went into hypothermia. Even Bruce was starting to lose consciousness, at times he didn't know if he was dreaming or awake. He desperately tried to find a way out of the dense fog, as long as he had a shred of life left, he would stay at the controls fighting. He looked at the seat to his right, Fran seemed to have lost consciousness and with effort hit him on the shoulder so he wouldn't fall asleep. If they fell asleep they would never wake up. Assessing the situation, perhaps it was best to fall asleep and let go. Falling into the frozen waters, death's agony could be dreadful. His eyelids were as heavy as lead and in his ears he heard a distant buzz. Bruce thought it was the end. The noise grew louder. It was familiar to him, like an old song, after a while he identified it, it was the sound of an engine and not just any engine, it was an Hirth HM60R/2 80 hp. He opened his eyes with effort and looked to the left where he heard the plane approaching. Out of the fog a biplane emerged and positioned itself in front of them, banking indicating for them to follow it. Bruce followed it until suddenly, as if going through a cotton cloud, they came out of the fog flying above the blue sky under a bright sun. When he looked ahead the Bücker Bü 131 Jungmann was no longer there. There was nothing but the clear blue sky above the darker blue of the ocean. He rubbed his eyes and heard the characteristic engine noise again, now much closer. He looked to his left and the old Bücker appeared at his side, almost touching the window with its wing. The pilot a blonde woman with very light green eyes, gave him a lovely smile, then brought her open hand to her temple in a military pilot's salute. She executed a wing drop maneuver and disappeared.

When he looked at the co-pilot's seat, Fran was looking at him seriously.

"Did you see the blonde woman who waved at us from the plane?" - He asked looking at Bruce as he rubbed his face as if just waking from a dream.

"I saw her. She's a good friend."

The sun charged the aircraft and all systems came back online. Lucrèce approached, with Maria leaning on her shoulder. She was much better, the fever was gone. The four survivors came together in a joyful hug.

****_INVADERS_****

****_The invasion has begun_****

****_The Day After Tomorrow_****

As the days went by, the infected disappeared, although most perished some were cured thanks to new medicines. They made contact with people of all nationalities, inhabitants from every corner of the world, who had survived the infection. On islands, in remote mountain villages and also in bunkers enduring underground. The hope of a new world opened up before them. The opportunity to start over from scratch. The science and technology of the old world, with the legacy of all of human history, on a planet where there was no longer a need to fight over resources. The cities, archaic monsters, were abandoned and small rural communities were created, where people of all races and nationalities lived together. The less pleasant tasks were carried out communally, sharing the work among everyone. In other words, if everyone recycles their own garbage, no one has to work collecting that of others. A world in which everyone could be whatever they wanted to be, artists, teachers and doctors. There are tastes for everything, sharing tasks and wealth, everyone could live happily. It wasn't necessary to implement birth control, couples realized they could be happy without needing to have ten children. The children learned a new language, a mix of all the others, this way everyone was connected, maintaining communication via the Internet.

Lucrèce and Francisco got married on the Faroe Islands and months later moved to France, although countries and borders no longer existed. The children of the new world would grow up without knowing the meaning of having a nationality, without knowing what a border is or the meaning of the word immigrant.

114

INVADERS

The invasion has begun

Jellyfish Invasion

Protocol for action in case of a viral pandemic similar to rabies

By Dr. Maria Garcia

1. State security forces, the army and police, will separate the population using containment barriers, dividing cities into sectors. To move from one area to another, the quarantine protocol must be followed. "No one can cross from one zone to another without complying with said protocol".
2. Qualified personnel, doctors, teachers, scientists and politicians who may be relevant to finding a solution, will be sent to small islands and large vessels.
3. Transportation will be carried out in secure vehicles, armored vans and tank-type vehicles.
4. International flights will be prohibited. To travel from one country to another, land borders must be crossed undergoing a quarantine period.
5. Personnel forming the special containment operations corps will wear adequate body armor with full helmet, mask with proper activated carbon filters, gloves and boots.
6. In case of confrontation, the use of weapons that do not cause bleeding is recommended, such as Tasers, avoiding bloodshed and spread of the virus.

7. If all of the above measures fail, it is recommended to drink as much alcohol as possible - drunks can pass for infected and live happily among them.

Did you love *Invaders the Invasion Has Begun?* Then you should read *Freak - The Circus of Horrors*[1] by Francisco Angulo de Lafuente!

[2]

Critics are hailing Francisco Angulo latest novel Freak as "a modern gothic masterpiece" (The New York Times) that is "impossible to put down" (Washington Post).

Set against the backdrop of a mysterious traveling circus, Freak chronicles the experiences of a group of extraordinary characters who possess uncanny abilities and physical anomalies that set them apart from mainstream society. Led by the enigmatic magician known only as "Nikola," the "freaks" of the circus unveil a riveting story of drama, suspense, romance, horror, and humanity.

As Angulo peels back the layers of his vividly drawn characters, he illuminates the struggles of those deemed abnormal and the cruelty

---

1. https://books2read.com/u/3nB8v6

2. https://books2read.com/u/3nB8v6

and wonder of human nature. Heart-wrenching, chilling and tender by turns, Freak explores discrimination, revenge, compassion and redemption with sensitivity and depth.

Hailed for its "spellbinding pace and tantalizing secrets" (Chicago Tribune), Freak conjures up a world that seduces readers into the rich inner lives of beings who are at once bizarre and deeply familiar. Through elegant prose alive with stunning imagery, Diaz has crafted a novel that will haunt you long after the final page.

The boy stared with wide-eyed wonder as the circus tents bloomed up from the misty dawn like giant mushrooms come to life. He clutched his guardian's hand tightly, scarcely believing he'd been allowed to attend the show. After so many whispered stories of sideshow freaks and death-defying acts, he would finally see the spectacle for himself.

As the sun burned off the morning fog, a kaleidoscope of sights, sounds and smells dazzled the boy's senses. Roars rumbled from animal cages while vendors sang out about sugared treats. Bold circus posters depicted fire-eaters, sword-swallowers, a wolfman, a bearded woman, a turtle boy and more. What strange creatures awaited him inside the striped big top?

The boy remembered his schoolmates jeering at him, calling him a "freak." But here, could the freaks walk openly, without shame? The idea filled him with awe.

A gruff voice interrupted his musings - it was time for the show to start. The boy hurried inside, clutching his ticket stub like a golden ticket. The tent flaps swept closed behind him with a whisper, and the lights dimmed...

As foreboding organ notes crept through the heavy air, the ringmaster stalked into the spotlight, cracked his whip, and proclaimed, "Ladies and gentlemen, welcome to the greatest show on earth!"

Read more at https://twitter.com/Francisco_Ecofa.

Also by Francisco Angulo de Lafuente

Eco-fuel-FA (ECOFA) A viable solution
El Olfateador нюхальщик
Los Mejores (The Best)
То,что Вы не должны делать ,чтобы стать писателем

Compañía N°12
Destino La Habana - Destination Havana
EL OLFATEADOR
La leyenda de los Tarazashi
LÁZARO RIP
Estrella fugaces en el cielo de verano
Commander Valentina Smirnova
Escapando del Infierno
Comandante Valentina Smirnova
Freak - El Circo de los Horrores
INVADERS La invasión ha comenzado
The Sniffer
Una boda gitana y un funeral escocés
Freak - The Circus of Horrors
Escaping from Hell
Shooting Stars in the Summer Sky
Cosas que no debes hacer si quieres ser escritor
Destination Havana
The Relic
Invaders the Invasion Has Begun

Watch for more at https://twitter.com/Francisco_Ecofa.

About the Author

Francisco Angulo Madrid, 1976

Enthusiast of fantasy cinema and literature and a lifelong fan of Isaac Asimov and Stephen King, Angulo starts his literary career by submitting short stories to different contests. At 17 he finishes his first book - a collection of poems – and tries to publish it. Far from feeling intimidated by the discouraging responses from publishers, he decides to push ahead and tries even harder.

In 2006 he published his first novel "The Relic", a science fiction tale that was received with very positive reviews. In 2008 he presented "Ecofa" an essay on biofuels, whereAngulorecounts his experiences in the research project he works on. In 2009 he published "Kira and the Ice Storm".A difficultbut very productive year, in2010 he completed "Eco-fuel-FA",a science book in English. He also worked on several literary projects: "The Best of 2009-2010", "The Legend of Tarazashi 2009-2010", "The Sniffer 2010", "Destination Havana 2010-2011" and "Company No.12".

He currently works as director of research at the Ecofa project. Angulo is the developer of the first 2nd generation biofuel obtained from organic waste fed bacteria. He specialises in environmental issues and science-fiction novels.

His expertise in the scientific field is reflected in the innovations and technological advances he talks about in his books, almost prophesying what lies ahead, as Jules Verne didin his time.

Francisco Angulo Madrid-1976

Gran aficionado al cine y a la literatura fantástica, seguidor de Asimov y de Stephen King, Comienza su andadura literaria presentando relatos cortos a diferentes certámenes. A los 17 años termina su primer libro, un poemario que intenta publicar sin éxito. Lejos de amedrentarse ante las respuestas desalentadoras de las editoriales, decide seguir adelante, trabajando con más ahínco.

Read more at https://twitter.com/Francisco_Ecofa.

9 798223 917441